JASON STARR

TOUGH LUCK

Jason Starr is the author of *Cold Caller, Nothing Personal, Fake I.D.,* and *Hard Feelings.* He lives with his wife and daughter in New York City. Visit his home page at www.jasonstarr.com.

TOUGH

LUCK

JASON STARR

VINTAGE CRIME/BLACK LIZARD

VINTAGE BOOKS

A DIVISION OF RANDOM HOUSE, INC.

NEW YORK

A VINTAGE CRIME/BLACK LIZARD ORIGINAL, JANUARY 2003

Library of Congress Cataloging-in-Publication Data
Starr, Jason.
Tough luck / Jason Starr.
p.   cm.
ISBN 0-375-72711-6 (pbk.)
1. New York (N.Y.)—Fiction. 2. Swindlers and swindling—Fiction.
3. Gambling—Fiction. I. Title.
PS3569.T336225 T68 2003
813'.54—dc21   2002066370

Book design by JoAnne Metsch
Author photograph © Julie Scholz

www.vintagebooks.com

Printed in the United States of America
10   9   8   7   6   5   4   3   2   1

For Chynna Skye

TOUGH

LUCK

1

WHEN THE BIG Italian-looking guy in the pin-striped suit came into Vincent's Fish Market on Flatbush Avenue and Avenue J, Mickey Prada put down the copy of the *Daily News* he'd been reading and said, "The usual, right?"

"You got it, kid," the big guy said, smiling.

As Mickey filled the order—a pound of cooked shrimp and a small container of cocktail sauce—the guy took out a piece of paper and held it up for Mickey to see.

"Can you believe this shit?" the guy said. "I gotta go into fuckin' court today."

The paper had a lot of writing on it, but all Mickey saw before the guy put it away were the big letters *OC* written in red in the corner.

"I can't believe they waste my time with this shit," the guy went on, shaking his head. "But I'll get off. I always do."

Mickey rang up the order. After he gave the guy his change from a fifty, the guy stuck out his hand and said, "By the way, name's Angelo. Angelo Santoro."

Mickey wiped his hand clean on his dirty white apron and shook Angelo's big hand.

"Mickey. Mickey Prada."

THAT NIGHT, MICKEY was at his friend Chris's, watching the Islanders-Flyers game on the new color set in Chris's bedroom. During a commercial, Mickey told Chris about Angelo Santoro and the court papers.

"Don't fuck with that guy, whatever you do," Chris said.

"What do you mean?" Mickey asked.

"OC, dickhead. You know what OC stands for, don't you?"

Mickey shook his head.

"Organized crime, moron. Your friend Angelo's a wiseguy."

"Come on," Mickey said.

"Trust me," Chris said. "I know what I'm talking about."

The next time Angelo came into the fish store, a couple of days later, Mickey took a closer look at him. It was hard to tell how old Angelo was because his hair was jet-black, probably colored with Brylcreem, but he looked forty, or maybe a couple of years older. And he definitely had a Mafia way about him. It wasn't just the slicked-back hair and the snazzy clothes—it was the way he acted, always half-smiling and walking with a strut.

Mickey was nicer than usual to Angelo—smiling, asking him how his day was, adding some extra shrimp to his container. Angelo was friendly too, talking about the election next month, predicting that Reagan would kick Mondale's ass.

At the register, while Mickey was ringing up the order, Angelo said, "So you're a football fan, huh, kid?"

"Yeah," Mickey said. "How'd you know?"

"Heard you talking the other day with the black kid who works here. So you think the Jets're gonna do it this year?"

"Hope so," Mickey said.

"It'll be tough," Angelo said, "the way the Fish're playing—seven and oh—but that O'Brien kid looks pretty good out there, and they got that great D. I got season tix you know."

"Really?" Mickey said.

"Yeah, had 'em since sixty-eight."

"You saw the Jets the year they won the Super Bowl?"

"Was at every game, including the big one."

"You were *there*?"

"January 12, 1969. The Orange Bowl, Miami, Florida. Fifth row, forty-yard line."

"Holy shit," Mickey said.

"Shoulda seen Namath that day, kid, hookin' up with Maynard and Sauer." Angelo pretended to throw a football. "Too bad his fuckin' knees went or he'd still be QBin'. Hey, I don't know if you're interested, but I can't use my tickets for the Jets-Giants game in December. If you wanna use 'em, you can."

"I don't know," Mickey said. "I mean I'd love to go, but I don't think I can afford it."

"Afford? Who said anything about afford? I'm *giving* you the tickets." Angelo grinned.

"That's okay," Mickey said. "I mean you don't have to do that."

"Hey, don't insult me," Angelo said, suddenly serious. "I said I want to give you the tickets, and I'm giving you the tickets. It's the least I could do for my favorite fish man."

"Okay," Mickey said. "I mean if you really wanna do that."

Angelo smiled widely again. "The game's not till December—I'm sure I'll see you a lot before then. I'll bring the tickets in with me one of these days."

"Thanks," Mickey said.

"You take it easy, now," Angelo said.

THE FOLLOWING MONDAY afternoon Mickey was working at the countertop behind the fish stands, cutting flounder fillets. After he scraped off the scales, he made one short cut under the front fin, just behind the gills, then a longer cut down to the tail. He did the same thing to the other side of the fish, then he scooped out the carcass, pushed the fillets off to the side, and started on the next one.

As Mickey was cutting flounder, Mrs. Ruiz came into the store.

"How are you today, Mrs. Ruiz?"

"Very good, Mickey."

"What can I get for you?"

"You got mussels?"

Mickey rolled up the sleeve on his right arm, flexed his biceps, and said, "Yep."

When Mrs. Ruiz left the store with her usual two pounds of mussels and two pounds of clams for her paella, Charlie came in from the back, holding a big boom box up on his shoulder.

"Turn that shit off," Mickey said.

"Come on," Charlie said, "even white people like this music."

"I'm serious," Mickey said.

Charlie lowered the volume.

"I forgot—you Italian," Charlie said. "You like that John Travolta, Bee Gees shit. On weekends you probably dress up like Deney Terrio and start crankin' the Donna Summer. Come on, it's the truth. You can't hide it."

Mickey couldn't help smiling as Charlie sang along, *"And don't ever come down . . . Freebase!"*

Charlie continued to sing as Mickey cut into another flounder.

"Mickey Prada, how's it going?"

Mickey turned around and saw Angelo standing there on the other side of the fish stands, wearing one of his pin-striped suits. Angelo hadn't been to the fish store in about a week, and Mickey was surprised Angelo remembered his name.

"How's it goin'?" Mickey said. "Hey, Angelo, this is Charlie."

Charlie and Angelo said hi to each other, then Charlie lowered the music and went to help another customer who'd just come in.

"You know why I'm here," Angelo said to Mickey.

"Coming right up," Mickey said.

As Mickey was putting the cooked shrimp into a one-pound container, Angelo said, "Prada. That's not Sicilian, is it?"

"Nah, my grandfather was from up north," Mickey said.

"Milano?"

"Somewhere around there."

"Eh, what's the difference?" Angelo said. "North, south, you're still from the old country, that's what counts. So tell me something else, kid. What do you want to do with your life?"

"What do you mean?"

"I mean here you are, working at a fish store. You go to school?"

"I'm taking a year off, then I'm gonna go to college at Baruch in the city."

"College?" Angelo said like he'd never heard the word before. "What're you gonna learn there?"

"I want to be an accountant," Mickey said.

"Accountant?" Angelo said. "You're not gonna become an IRS agent, are you?"

Mickey laughed. "Nah, I'm just gonna get a job for a company. You know, Ernst and Young or someplace like that."

"Yeah, that sounds good," Angelo said, "I guess. But if you're ever lookin' for something else to do, you come talk to me, all right? If you're good with numbers I can set you up at something, you'll make a good living for yourself. You know anything about numbers?"

"You mean *betting* numbers?" Mickey said.

Angelo nodded.

"I know a little," Mickey said. "I mean I don't play the numbers myself but—"

"That's okay," Angelo said, "better you don't. The odds of hitting the number are what, a thousand-somethin' to one? I got a better chance of dying today than I got of hitting the number. I'm talking about the *other* side of the business.

You're good with math, you can work on the odds, that kind of thing, right?"

"Thanks," Mickey said. "But I think I'll probably just keep working here . . . until I start school again."

"Hey, it's up to you," Angelo said. "You do whatever you want to do. I'm just saying you're a good kid—I think you're gonna go places. I don't think you need school to get there, neither. I think you can get there right now if you wanted to. But you think about it, you let me know, okay?"

"I will," Mickey said.

Mickey weighed Angelo's shrimp then closed the container. At the register, Angelo said, "So who do you like in the game tonight?"

"The game?" Mickey said.

"Monday Night Football."

"Oh, the Seahawks," Mickey said.

"The *Seahawks?*" Angelo said. "Come on, Dan Fouts's got the best arm in football. The Chargers are a fuckin' lock tonight."

"I don't know," Mickey said. "The 'Hawks beat up the Chargers last time pretty good, and now they're getting a point. You gotta go with the 'Hawks."

"Oh, so you like to *bet* on football, huh?" Angelo said, smiling.

"I just bet a few dollars with a bookie every once in a while," Mickey said. "It's no big deal."

"You gotta be careful," Angelo said. "Don't get me wrong—I like a little action every now and then myself, but you don't wanna get in too deep. Guys I know lose their families, lose everything from gambling. One guy I know, old friend of mine, liked playing the numbers. Bet a few bucks a week, thought, What's the worst that could happen? Year later he's broke, his wife and kids're gone, he has nothing."

"That won't happen to me," Mickey said.

Angelo stared at Mickey for a few seconds, then said, "You're a smart kid, you know that? Got a good head on your shoulders is what I mean. Do me a favor, my bookie's out of town this week. Can you put in a little action for me tonight too?"

Mickey hesitated then he said, "I usually don't put in other people's bets. No offense but—"

"But in my case you'll make an exception, right?" Angelo smiled.

"Sure," Mickey said. "I mean I don't see why not. What do you want?"

"What'd you say the line was?"

"San Diego minus one."

"What're they, giving money tonight? Gimme ten times Chargers."

"That's fifty dollars," Mickey said.

"I know what it is," Angelo said. "It's not a problem, is it?"

"I guess not," Mickey said. "I mean I usually don't bet that much. . . ."

"Like I said, I'd call my own bookie but he's away this week on vacation—West Palm Beach. So you'll put the bet in for me, right? Just as a favor."

Mickey hesitated, remembering what Chris told him about not getting involved with the mob, but he couldn't think of a way to say no. Besides, this wasn't really getting involved.

"Yeah, sure," he said. "No problem."

"Good," Angelo said.

"But the thing is," Mickey said, "I don't know what my bookie's line is. I mean, the Chargers might be laying more than one point or—"

"It don't matter," Angelo said, smiling. "I trust you, kid."

ABOUT HALF AN hour before kickoff, Mickey called his bookie and put in Angelo's bet. The line had drifted to one and a half points, but it didn't matter because the Seahawks crushed the Chargers 24–zip. Mickey won his own "five time," or twenty-five-dollar bet, but Angelo lost fifty-five bucks—fifty for the bet and five for the bookie's vig.

When Angelo came into the store the next day, he didn't mention football. He just bullshitted with Mickey about the cold weather in New York and how he wanted to move to Miami someday.

Ringing up Angelo's order, Mickey said, "So, did you see the game last night?" hoping Angelo would hand over the fifty-five bucks.

"Yeah, I saw it," Angelo said. "Tough loss, huh, kid?" Then he said, "So long," and left the store with his shrimp.

AT AROUND NOON on Wednesday Angelo came into the fish store, wearing a black sweater, black pants, and shiny black shoes.

"Mickey Prada," he said, smiling. "How's my favorite fish man?"

As Mickey filled Angelo's order, Angelo talked about how they should put Reagan's picture on the dollar bill someday and how the city needed to get Koch out of office. He didn't mention anything about football until right before he left when he said, "Don't forget, I'm giving you those Jets-Giants tickets, kid."

Angelo didn't come to the store on Thursday, but he showed up on Friday at his usual time. After he ordered his pound of cooked shrimp, he said to Mickey, "Oh, I meant to ask you, you got the lines on Sunday's games?"

"I didn't call yet," Mickey said, hoping Angelo wouldn't want to bet again.

"Yeah? Well, when you do call, put this in for me." Angelo slid a folded-up piece of paper across the counter.

"I was gonna say something to you about that," Mickey said. "I need to pay off my bookie before I can put in any more action for you."

"But the Chargers lost," Angelo said.

"I know," Mickey said.

"So what're you telling me?" Angelo said. "You saying you won't give me a chance to get even?"

"It's not *me*," Mickey said.

"Look, I don't have time for a headache right now, all right?" Angelo said. "I'm in the middle of taking care of some trouble with this landscaping company. They moved in on our turf and now I have to go and straighten things out. So you can imagine I got more important shit on my mind than some fucking fifty-dollar football bet. So just be a good kid and put this action in for me before you start to get me upset."

Mickey didn't look at the paper until Angelo was gone. Angelo had written down bets for four different games. All together the new bets came to $138.

Charlie, who had been working at the other end of the store, came over to Mickey and said, "What was that all about?"

"Nothing," Mickey said, and he walked through the doors to the back of the store to be alone.

Mickey didn't know what to do. He didn't want to put in any more action for Angelo, but he didn't want to get stuck for the money, either. If he didn't place the bets and the teams won, Angelo would expect his winnings, and Mickey didn't want to have to pay him out of his own pocket.

Finally, Mickey decided to put the bets in. It was only $138 and Angelo was probably good for it.

On Sunday, Mickey rooted for Angelo's teams, but it didn't help. Only one of Angelo's teams won, and he now owed a total of $140.

Monday afternoon, Angelo came into the store while Charlie was on his lunch break, and there were no other customers around. He told Mickey a story about a friend of his, "another made guy," but he didn't mention anything about the bets. Then, when Mickey was checking out Angelo at the register, Angelo said, "Jesus, I almost forgot," and he reached into the inside pocket of his suit jacket, and Mickey saw the handle of a black handgun sticking out. From behind the gun Angelo removed a folded-up piece of paper.

"I don't care what the lines are," Angelo said, handing the paper to Mickey, "just put this in for me, will ya, kid?"

Angelo left the store, lighting a cigarette like he didn't have a worry in the world. Mickey looked at the sheet of paper:

> 20 TIMES FALCONS IF OVER
>
> 20 TIMES FALCONS
>
> 20 TIMES OVER

"Shit," Mickey said.

Including the vig the new bets came to $330. If the bets lost, Angelo would be $470 in the hole.

Mickey couldn't afford to lay out so much money—he only had about two thousand dollars in the bank, and that was for expenses while he went to college in the fall—but he knew he had to put the bets in anyway. If the bets won, Angelo would expect his money and Mickey would have no choice but to pay him.

At eight o'clock, Mickey called Artie to find out the line on the game. He had known Artie forever—at least ten years. When was growing up, his father used to take him to the racetrack almost every Saturday; Artie was one of the regulars at Aqueduct, hanging out on the ground floor under the tote board near the Bagel Nook. Artie wasn't a bookie himself; he worked for a bookie, a guy named Nick whom Mickey had only met a couple of times. In junior high and high school, Mickey hustled football betting sheets for Artie in all of his classes. The sheets had pro and college games with odds stacked heavily in favor of the house. Artie paid

Mickey 10 percent on all the profits, which usually meant about fifty bucks a week.

"Line's twelve, forty-three," Artie said. "Been drifting up all day. Everybody loves the 'Skins tonight."

Artie said the phone lines were busy and he couldn't talk long, so Mickey put in Angelo's bets on the Falcons right away.

"Who is this Angelo, anyway?" Artie asked.

Mickey was embarrassed to tell Artie that he barely knew the guy.

"Friend of mine," Mickey said.

"And he has this kind of dough?"

"Yeah," Mickey said confidently.

"If Angelo loses, he knows he's gotta pay by Friday."

"He knows."

"You sure?"

"Sure I'm sure."

That night John Riggins rushed for one hundred yards, and the Washington Redskins beat the Atlanta Falcons 27–14. All of Angelo's bets had lost, and now he owed Mickey's bookie 470 bucks.

The next morning Mickey was in a shitty mood. When Mrs. Ruiz came in and said, "You got mussels?" Mickey didn't feel like playing the game, and he snapped, "Of course we got mussels. How much you want?" Distracted the rest of the day, he screwed up a couple of orders—giving a lady fluke fillets instead of flounder fillets, giving some guy butterfish who'd asked for kingfish, filling a bag with mussels instead of clams. Mickey's boss, Harry, warned

Mickey to get his head out of his ass or he was going to send him on a "permanent vacation."

Harry Giordano co-owned Vincent's Fish Market with his brother Vincent, who lived in Florida. Harry had a huge beer gut, a thick handlebar mustache, and was one of the biggest morons Mickey had ever met. Mickey figured Vincent must have put up the money for the store, because there was no way Harry could have been smart enough to save up the money to start a business on his own. Besides, it was called Vincent's Fish Market, not Harry's Fish Market, or even Giordano's Fish Market.

When Mickey started working at Vincent's, he didn't think he would last at the job for more than a couple of weeks. Mickey was sensitive about the size of his nose— sometimes he would stare at himself in the three-way mirrors in the dressing room at Alexander's, amazed at how big it was—and Harry always made jokes about it, especially when other people were around. One day, a guy was placing an order, and Mickey was talking to someone else and didn't hear what the guy was saying. Harry said, "Hey, Pinocchio, take this guy's order." Another time the same thing happened, and Harry said, "Hey, Big Bird, get your beak out of the clouds, will ya?" The worst part was that, since Harry was his boss, Mickey could never talk back to him. Mickey was dying to crack jokes about Harry's big beer gut, but Mickey knew Harry would fire him if he did. Mickey could have found some other job, but he was making decent money at the fish store—seven-fifty an hour—and the location was convenient, only six blocks from his house. So every time Harry insulted him, Mickey just ignored it, hoping Harry would eventually get tired of being a dick and leave him alone.

Harry had no schedule. Usually he just came to the store to open and close, but once in a while he stuck around all day.

Today Harry left at about eleven and, since there were hardly any customers in the store, Mickey hung out most of the time, reading the *Daily News* and talking to Charlie.

At one o'clock, Charlie left for lunch. Then, at around one-fifteen, Angelo strolled in.

"The usual," he said to Mickey. Then he said, "You know what? I think I'll mix it up for once. How're the fried-fish sandwiches?"

"Pretty good," Mickey said.

"Yeah? Lemme get two of 'em," Angelo said.

As Mickey fried the cod fillets on the skillet, he felt the sweat building on his back. He didn't care if Angelo was in the mob and carried a gun. He wanted his 470 bucks.

"About those bets you made," Mickey said to Angelo as he was putting the sandwiches in a paper bag. "You know your figure is up to four-seventy now."

"Is that what it is?" Angelo said casually. "Now I see why you wanna be an accountant—you're good at keeping track of numbers."

Angelo blew his nose into a handkerchief then replaced the handkerchief inside the jacket pocket of his pin-striped suit.

Mickey smiled, only because he was nervous. He didn't think there was anything funny about possibly getting stuck owing $470.

"Anyway," Mickey said, "I'm kind of short on cash, and I was hoping I could, you know, see some of that money today."

"I'll get you the money," Angelo said. "Don't worry about it. What do you think, I'm a thief?"

Angelo glared at Mickey, then he took the bag of fish sandwiches and strutted toward the register. There were a couple of other people on line, but Mickey left them there and walked behind the counter to the front of the store, meeting Angelo.

"Sorry, Angelo, I really am, but I need to know like when you're planning to give me that money. It's not me, it's my bookie. He makes me keep a two-hundred-fifty-dollar pay-or-collect number, and you're already way over it. He said he needs his money by Friday."

"Needs?" Angelo said, his face suddenly pink. "Did I hear you say *needs?* I don't *need* to do anything except die. You got that?"

"Yes," Mickey said.

"I said I'll get you the money, didn't I?"

"When?"

"When I give it to you," Angelo said.

"No problem," Mickey said. "I don't care one way or another. It's not me, it's just my bookie, like I was saying. I mean to him you're just a name, like any other name and—"

"You tell your bookie, Angelo Santoro makes up the rules when it comes to his bets, and nobody else. Before your bookie sees any money, I want a chance to get even. I'm going to the Knicks game Thursday night. Gimme a hundred times Knicks."

"That's another five hundred fifty dollars," Mickey said.

"I know what the fuck it is," Angelo said.

"I can't put in any more action for you," Mickey said.

"Can't?" Angelo said. "I don't think you heard me right, because I know you wouldn't tell me 'can't.' You *better* put that action in for me unless you wanna kiss your skinny little ass good-bye."

ON THURSDAY NIGHT Mickey wasn't in the mood to go bowling, but he had no choice. Mickey, Chris, and two of Chris's friends, Ralph and Filippo, were in a money league at Gil Hodges Lanes in Canarsie. They each had put up fifty dollars at the start of the season, with a chance to win two hundred apiece if their team won the championship.

Mickey arrived at the bowling alley with his bowling ball, wearing his uniform—an extra-large white T-shirt with the team's name, "The Studs," written in script across the chest. Chris had come up with the team's name, and Mickey always felt like a big idiot whenever he wore the shirt.

Chris, Filippo, and Ralph were waiting for Mickey by the shoe-rental counter. Chris and Filippo worked together, unloading and shelving groceries at Waldbaum's on Nostrand and Kings Highway, and Ralph and Filippo were good friends; but Mickey was only friends with Chris.

Chris used to be a shy, quiet kid who never got into any trouble, then his father took off when he was ten years old. His mother, who'd always liked to drink, became an alcoholic, and Chris started getting into fights at school, getting suspended all the time. One night, during the summer after

sixth grade, Chris and some other kids tried to rob a drug-
store on Avenue U. One kid pulled a knife and slashed the
owner's face, and Chris was sent to juvenile detention for
two years. When he came out he was still short, but he had
big, bulging muscles and he became one of the most popular kids in the neighborhood. He dropped out of high school
during eleventh grade when he got the job at Waldbaum's.

Filippo was tall, about six-two, and he'd had the same
military-style crew cut since he was a few years old. When
he wasn't wearing his Studs T-shirt, he dressed like a real
cugine, in white tank tops and gold chains. Filippo and
Mickey had never gotten along. In kindergarten, Filippo
always teased Mickey and he convinced other kids not to
like him. In elementary school, whenever Filippo passed
Mickey in the hallway, he would slap him on the head or
punch him in the arm as hard as he could, and he even beat
him up a few times after school. In junior high, Filippo
busted the lock on Mickey's locker, just for the hell of it,
and one day in gym class he snuck up behind Mickey and
pulled down his gym shorts, and all the girls laughed. In
high school, Filippo continued to pick on Mickey all the
time, and Mickey was glad when Filippo dropped out of
school to work with Chris.

Ralph was an older guy, around thirty. Mickey didn't
know much about him except that he had done time at
Attica for armed robbery and had gotten out about two years
ago. He was a big guy, with more fat than muscle, and he
had clumps of black hair on his back and shoulders that
spread out over the neckline of his Studs T-shirt. His lower
lip always hung down, exposing the tip of his tongue and his

crooked bottom teeth, and he made gurgling sounds in the
back of his throat when he breathed. Ralph was friends with
Filippo, so when Chris started hanging out with Filippo he
started hanging out with Ralph too. Ralph had never said a
word to Mickey, and Mickey had only heard him speak a
few times, to Filippo and Chris. Mickey thought there was
something seriously wrong with Ralph, but whenever Mickey
asked Chris about it, Chris always said, "Nah, Ralph's just
like that."

Mickey's bowling average was 145, but he was so distracted in the first game, thinking about his trouble with
Angelo, that he only bowled a 97. Afterward, Filippo said to
him, "Hey, Mickey Mouse, what's wrong, you got a dick up
your ass?"

In the first two frames of the second game, Mickey didn't
get a single mark, and in the third frame he threw two gut-
ter balls. After the second ball bounced off the alley, Filippo
yelled, "That's it! I don't want this faggot on the team no
more! He fuckin' sucks!"

Mickey bowled two strikes on his next two balls and
ended the game with a respectable 134. Between games, he
went into the bathroom.

"You all right tonight, buddy?" Chris said, coming in
behind him.

"Fine," Mickey said.

"You sure?" Chris said. "I don't know, you seem kind of
out of it. What's the matter, your old man acting up again?"

"Nah, it's not that." Mickey didn't feel like talking about
his problem with Angelo, but then he decided it might be
good to get some advice.

So Mickey told Chris about the bets he'd put in for Angelo and how much Angelo had lost. When Mickey finished, Chris, who was trying to pop a zit on his forehead in the mirror above the sink, said, "Didn't I tell you to be careful with that guy?"

"That's not the point," Mickey said. "The point is he lost this money, and I don't know what the hell to do about it."

"That's a tough one," Chris said. "I mean, on the one hand, the guy owes you the money. On the other hand, you can't fuck with the mob. I guess you gotta pay."

"But I don't have that kind of money."

"What do you mean? I thought you've been putting away."

"No fuckin' way, I've been saving that money for college since I was nine years old. I'm not giving it away now, not for this bullshit."

"Then I guess you gotta hope Angelo comes through," Chris said. "How's my hair look?"

When Chris and Mickey left the bathroom, they passed two girls, walking in the opposite direction. They were wearing tight jeans and tube tops, and their hair was big and frizzy. The odor of their strong perfumes made Mickey nauseous.

"Jesus, you see the knockers on that short one?" Chris said. "What a fuckin' set."

"What if he doesn't pay?" Mickey said.

"What? You don't like that?" Chris said, still staring at the girl.

"I don't have that kind of money to shell out," Mickey said.

"You want to know what I'd do?" Chris said. "I'd sit down

and talk to Artie. You know the guy a long time, right? Explain him the situation. Maybe you can work out some sort of payment plan or something. . . . Man, I gotta get laid tonight."

Another girl passed by, and Chris turned around to look at her ass.

"Hello, Lucy," he said. The girl kept walking, then he said, "Karen . . . Lisa . . . Amy . . . Barbara . . . Helen . . ."

Finally, the girl turned around, sticking up her middle finger.

"Your name's Helen, I knew it," Chris said. "Marry me, Helen. Come on, have my babies!"

Chris laughed, his tongue hanging out of his mouth.

"Do me a favor," Mickey said, "don't say anything to the other guys about this."

"About what?" Chris said.

"About Angelo," Mickey said.

"Why not?" Chris asked.

"Because I just don't want you to."

"Whatever," Chris said.

Mickey bowled an 89 in the third game, the lowest score on the team. Now if The Studs didn't win next week, there would be no chance of finishing in first place.

While Mickey was turning in his bowling shoes at the counter, he heard Filippo say to Chris, "I don't want that fuckin' faggot on the team no more."

"He'll get better," Chris said.

"He fuckin' sucks," Filippo said. "My grandmother in a wheelchair can bowl better than that pussy."

Ralph was looking at Mickey as if he wanted to kill him,

his left eye narrowed and his lower lip hanging down farther than ever.

"Don't worry about them," Chris whispered to Mickey. "They're just fuckin' retards." Then Chris said out loud, "Hey, you wanna come out with us tonight? We're gonna hit some tit joints in the city, and then we're gonna cruise the West Side for whores. Come on, if you wanna be on The Studs, you gotta act like one."

"No thanks," Mickey said.

"You're wasting your time," Filippo said to Chris. "I told you a million times, the guy's a fuckin' flame thrower. He saw a naked girl, he wouldn't know what to do with her. Ain't that right, Mick?"

"Have a good time," Mickey said to Chris, and walked away.

Later, driving down Ralph Avenue in his beat-up '76 Pinto, Mickey turned on the radio to an all-news station. The sportscaster came on and said that the Chicago Bulls and their rookie guard Michael Jordan had beaten the Knicks 121–106, meaning that Angelo now owed Mickey's bookie 1,020 bucks.

Mickey pounded the dashboard with the bottom of his fist as he stepped on the gas.

2

WHEN MICKEY ARRIVED at his apartment all the lights were out and his father wasn't home. Mickey hoped this didn't mean his old man was out wandering the streets again.

A few months ago, Sal Prada didn't come home one night, and Mickey had to call the cops. They finally found Sal the next morning, sleeping on a park bench in Bay Ridge, the neighborhood where he grew up. It was so humiliating to have the cop car pull up in front of the house with all the neighbors standing outside in their T-shirts and robes to see what was going on.

Mickey and his father lived in a small, narrow apartment on the second floor of a two-family house on Albany Avenue. There were two rooms in the apartment—Mickey's at one end of the hallway and his father's at the other end. In between there was a tiny kitchen and a bathroom barely big enough for a toilet, sink, and shower stall. Mickey couldn't wait to move out. He had hoped to find his own place this year, when he was supposed to start college, but he had put all of his plans on hold one night last July when his father collapsed at the dinner table. At first, Mickey thought it had something to do with his Alzheimer's, which had been getting worse over the past few years, but it turned out Sal had suffered a mild stroke. Sal didn't have any savings or pension—all he got were his monthly Social Security checks, which weren't much because he'd worked most of his life off the books. The doctors at the hospital suggested that Sal move to a nursing home or at least get a home attendant, but Sal refused. Although Sal had never been a good father, Mickey didn't want him to rot away in a home, so he put off school and started working full-time at the fish store. Mickey figured he could at least pay the rent and bills, which was all his father had ever done for him. He didn't want to get into debt with student loans, and he hoped that by next year he'd have enough money in his savings to afford expenses while he went to school during the day and worked part-time on nights and weekends.

After Mickey munched on some leftover pepperoni and anchovy pizza in the fridge, he went into his room and locked the door. He'd had the same furniture in his room since he was a kid—a dresser, a night table, a springy single bed in the corner, a black-and-white TV set with a busted picture tube so everything always looked grainy and shadowed. A poster of Reggie Jackson when he was on the Yankees hung behind Mickey's bed, and on the wall across from his bed was the poster of Farrah Fawcett-Majors smiling widely, her nipples showing through her bathing suit. Another poster, of Steve Cauthen atop Affirmed after winning the seventy-eight Derby, was attached to the back of his closet door.

Lying in bed, Mickey watched the end of the Knicks game, then he watched *The Odd Couple* and *The Honeymooners*. He had seen the episodes so many times that he knew all the lines by heart, and he didn't laugh or even smile at the jokes.

At midnight, Sal still wasn't home, Mickey was going to give it another half an hour, until *Letterman* went on, and then he heard the side door opening and his father's slow footsteps coming upstairs.

When Sal entered the apartment, Mickey was waiting in the hallway. People always told Mickey that he looked like his father, but Mickey hoped this wasn't true because he had always thought his father was the ugliest man alive. Sal had a small bald head, a huge Italian schnoz, big ears that stuck out, and he wore glasses that made his right eye look about twice the size of his left. Sal used to be taller than Mickey, but Mickey had grown late, in high school, and Sal had shrunk. Now Mickey had a good four inches on his old man.

"Where the hell've you been?" Mickey asked.

"What do you mean?" Sal said, almost yelling. He'd always talked loud, since Mickey could remember, even though there was nothing wrong with his hearing. "I took a walk. What, I can't take a fuckin' walk?"

Sal went to hang up his trench coat in the hall closet. It took him about ten seconds to figure out how to turn the handle on the closet door, and Mickey didn't go over to help. Finally, the old man put away his coat and then he headed past Mickey, down the narrow hallway to his bedroom.

Following his father, Mickey said, "You can't just disappear like that. I was gonna call the cops."

"The cops? Why would you call the cops?"

"Because I thought you got lost again."

"Lost? Why would I get lost? I've been living in Brooklyn seventy-five years. I know this city better than anybody."

"It's not a city."

"What?"

"Brooklyn's not a city, it's a borough."

"What the fuck're you talking about?"

"So where were you, anyway?"

"Shopping."

"Shopping? Where were you shopping?"

"What do you mean, the supermarket on Kings Highway."

"What supermarket on Kings Highway?"

"What do you mean? . . . Bohack's."

"Bohack's? There's no Bohack's on Kings Highway."

"What the hell're you talking about, Mi . . . Mi . . . Mi . . ."

"Mickey."

"I know your goddamn name. What, you think I can't find a fucking supermarket? I've been living in Brooklyn seventy-five years. I know this city better than anybody."

"Wha'd you buy?" Mickey asked. "I don't see any food."

Sal looked around.

"I must've put the bag down already in the kitchen. There's a lot of food in there, but don't eat it up all at once. It has to last all week. I bought ham and bologna and chicken salad. But save the chicken salad for your mother. You know she likes it."

"Mom's dead," Mickey said.

"Dead!" Sal shouted. "What the hell are you talking about?"

"She died in a hit and run fifteen years ago on the BQE, remember?"

"I know she's dead," Sal said, suddenly angry. "Jesus Christ, why don't you leave me the hell alone?"

Mickey had had enough.

"Good night, Dad."

"Where you going?"

"Bed."

"You wanna go to the track Saturday? I'll give you twenty to play with."

Mickey lay in bed with the lights off. Watching the occasional shadows on the ceiling from the headlights of cars passing by on Albany Avenue, he eventually fell asleep.

3

MICKEY'S ROOM WAS still dark when the phone rang. Without getting out of bed, he reached onto the floor and lifted the receiver.

"Hello," he mumbled.

"Pinocchio, get the marbles out of your mouth."

Mickey recognized Harry's voice.

"Yeah," Mickey said, his eyes closing again.

"Sorry to call you so early," Harry said, but Mickey could tell he wasn't really sorry. Harry was the type who enjoyed waking people up from deep sleeps. "We got a little problem today at the store and I need your help."

Harry explained that one of the freezers in the store had broken down last night and all the fish inside spoiled. The next delivery from the Fulton Fish Market wasn't for a few days, so Harry needed Mickey to come with him to Sheepshead Bay and buy fish straight off the boats.

"What time is it?" Mickey asked.

"Five o'clock," Harry said. "Be by the store in a half hour, will ya?"

"Yeah, yeah, all right," Mickey said, his eyes closing.

Mickey fell asleep then woke up again at five-fifteen. Without showering, he walked from his house to the fish store along the dark empty streets. Harry was waiting in the truck. When Mickey got in they said, "Morning," to each other, and they didn't say anything else until Harry pulled up in front of a deli on Flatbush and said, "Want some coffee?" and Mickey said, "Sure." Harry stood outside the car, waiting, then Mickey realized he wanted money. Mickey gave Harry a buck and then, when Harry was out of earshot, Mickey said, "Cheap fuck."

The coffee barely lifted Mickey's eyelids. Mickey and Harry arrived at Sheepshead Bay and had to wait about half an hour, with the rest of the buyers, until the fishing boats started to come into port. There was still mist over the bay, and the sun was just starting to rise; it was turning into a cool, breezy fall morning.

Staring at the boats and the docks, Mickey remembered all the times when he was eight and nine years old and he went out fishing with Chris and Chris's father. They were some of the only times in Mickey's life that he felt like a normal kid, doing the things normal kids did. The nights before, Mickey was so excited he could hardly sleep. Then, at five o'clock, he would go down to meet Chris and Mr. Turner. They would have an extra fishing pole for Mickey to use, and they'd drive down to Sheepshead Bay and take one of the boats. One time, Mickey caught a twenty-five pound striped bass. Well, he didn't really *catch* it. His line got tangled with some guy's line on the other side of the boat, and when the guy reeled both lines in, the fish was on Mickey's hook. Mickey still looked at the picture sometimes—Chris and him standing in front of the fishing boat, both smiling, holding up the huge fish between them.

The fishing boats pulled into the docks, and buyers from restaurants and fish stores all over Brooklyn lined up to buy the day's catch. Harry bought some fluke, flounder, striped bass, porgies, bluefish, and blackfish. At about a quarter to seven, they headed back to the fish store, Harry listening to some radio station that seemed to play Frank Sinatra every other song.

MICKEY AND CHARLIE unloaded the truck and then Harry left for the morning. Mickey had only gotten about four hours sleep, and it was hitting him hard. Even the Run-D.M.C. cassette Charlie was blasting on his boom box couldn't keep Mickey from feeling exhausted.

After putting ice on the stands, Mickey and Charlie washed the new whole fish and laid them on top of the ice, then they added the older fish they had stored in boxes in the refrigerator overnight. After they put out the shellfish in their own stands, they rested for a few minutes until the store opened for business at ten o'clock.

All morning, and especially around noon, every time the bell above the door rang, Mickey looked over, hoping to see Angelo. But when the lunch crowd started thinning out, around one-thirty, Mickey knew Angelo wasn't going to show.

At around two-o'clock, Harry returned to the store and said to Mickey, "Well, I feel great. I went home and slept like a baby for four hours." He stretched in an overexaggerated way and then went to the back of the store.

Mickey was cursing Harry under his breath when the bell above the door rang and a girl walked in. She had big curly brown hair with short straight bangs and was wearing tight faded jeans and a white sweatshirt coming off of one shoulder. She might have been about ten pounds overweight and her skin was broken out on her cheeks, but she was still one of the best-looking girls Mickey had ever seen.

"Why don't you take a picture, it'll last longer?"

Mickey looked over his shoulder and saw Charlie standing there, smiling.

"What are you talking about?" Mickey said.

"Ah, come on, man, who you kiddin'?" Charlie said. "I know you was just checkin' that girl out."

"What girl?" Mickey said.

"What girl?" Charlie said. "That's funny, man. Come on, what you waitin' for, an invitation? Go talk to her."

"Why?" Mickey said.

"Yo, just go for it, man. She's *still* checkin' you out."

"Sure she is."

"Why would I lie to you? Her eyes was just goin' up and down, lookin' at you like you a piece of prime rib on the rack. You gotta go take her order, anyway—why not get her phone number while you at it?"

Mickey knew Charlie was just egging him on. The girl was looking at the fish on the stands, deciding what to get.

"Are you gonna take the young lady's order or are you

just gonna let her stand there all day on her pretty little feeties?"

Harry had come out from the back, and he was standing behind Mickey with his hands on his hips.

Mickey noticed the girl's green eyes.

"Sorry, can I help you?" Mickey asked.

"Yes," the girl said, "can I have two pounds of flounder fillets and that striped bass right there?"

She pointed.

"You want the bass whole or in fillets?" Mickey asked.

"Whole," the girl said.

"You want me to cut off the head and tail?"

"Yes, please."

"You got it."

As Mickey was cutting the bass, he turned back toward the girl, looking at her legs in those tight jeans, wondering how she got them on, when he felt the pain in his right index finger. He looked at his finger, surprised to see how much blood was flowing out of it.

"Fuck," Mickey said.

Harry, at the other end of the counter, looked over.

"Jesus," Harry said. "What the hell's wrong with you?"

"The knife slipped," Mickey said.

"Slipped?" Harry said. "Don't you know how to cut a fucking fish?"

Now there was blood all over the counter and on the fish.

"Are you okay?" the girl asked.

"Yeah," Mickey said. "Fine." He didn't care about his finger, he just couldn't believe he'd made such a fool of himself.

"Look what you did," Harry said to Mickey. "You know how much this costs? Go clean this up—right now."

Mickey wound up his finger in the corner of his apron, then he went toward the kitchen, mumbling, "Fuck you."

"What was that?" Harry said.

"Nothing," Mickey said.

"I thought I heard you say something," Harry said.

"I didn't say anything," Mickey said.

Charlie must have come out from the back in time to hear what had happened because Charlie said to Harry, "It wasn't his fault."

"Was I talking to you, Budinsky?" Harry said. "Why don't you get back to work and mind your own fuckin' business, all right?"

"I just think that shit ain't right," Charlie said. "The knife slipped—it was an accident."

Mickey had stopped near the entrance to the back. As Charlie and Harry continued to argue, the girl came over toward Mickey and said, "Is it very deep?"

"It's not too bad," Mickey said.

Looking at Mickey's finger, the girl cringed. "Ooh, that looks bad. You might need stitches."

"It'll be okay."

"You better wash it out and put peroxide on it."

"Yeah, you're probably right," Mickey said.

Mickey went through the doors to the back of the store, to the bathroom and washed out the wound in the sink. In the dusty cabinet above the sink, there was no peroxide, but there was an old box of little Band-Aids. Mickey used a few of the bandages to cover the wound on his finger, but they didn't stop the bleeding. Maybe the girl was right about needing stitches.

With his hand around the injured finger, putting pressure on it, Mickey left the bathroom. Charlie had returned from the front of the store, but he looked angry and upset. He started cleaning the knives and cutting boards in the sink.

"Thanks for sticking up for me like that," Mickey said. "But you didn't have to do that."

"Hey, somebody had to say something," Charlie said. "That shit was wrong."

"Yeah, but you know nothing you say's gonna help."

"You're right," Charlie said. "Harry's just a fuckin' asshole, and he treats us like we the shit that comes outta it."

"Watch out," Mickey said. "He might hear you."

"I don't give a shit if the man hears me or not," Charlie said. "Let him hear me."

Mickey returned to the main part of the store, through the swinging doors. He wanted to talk to the girl again and apologize for the big scene he had caused, but he saw that she was gone. Only Harry was in the store, sitting on a stool by the cash register.

"What're you doing, standing there?" Harry said to Mickey. "Go clean up your mess."

Mickey hesitated then took a moist rag and started cleaning up the blood.

"What happened to that girl?" Mickey asked.

"What girl?" Harry said.

"The one who was just here."

"Oh, *her*. What do you think happened to her? She left. You probably disgusted her."

Harry laughed, walking away, then he turned back toward Mickey and said, "Why do you want to know, anyway?"

"Know what?" Mickey said, although he knew exactly what Harry meant.

"Come on," Harry said, "a pretty girl like that would never go for a guy like you, and you know it."

Harry started laughing again, belly-laughing, as if he thought he was the funniest guy in the world. Mickey finished cleaning up, pretending to ignore him.

Mickey knew Harry was just being a prick, but he also knew it was true—the girl probably didn't like him. She'd just acted nice because his finger was bleeding. If he hadn't cut his finger, she probably wouldn't have said a word.

Later in the day, Mickey's finger still looked bad, and he decided he definitely needed stitches. Before he left work, at around seven o'clock, he called his father to tell him he would be home late because he had to go to the emergency room. As usual, he wasn't sure if his father understood him. Suddenly angry and frustrated, Mickey hung up.

Mickey walked about ten blocks to Kings Highway Hospital and had to wait over an hour before a doctor would see him. The doctor sewed four stitches into Mickey's finger and told him the stitches would have to stay in for two weeks.

On his way home, Mickey stopped at John's Pizzeria on Flatbush and bought a pepperoni pie and two sodas. His father was waiting for him by the door when he walked in.

"Where the hell've you been?" Sal Prada asked.

Ignoring his father, Mickey put the pizza on the kitchen table then went into his room and changed out of his dirty

work clothes into clean jeans and a Rangers jersey with
"ESPOSITO 77" written across the back.

Mickey left his bedroom and went into the kitchen where
his father was sitting at the table eating a slice of pizza.
Mickey took one of the slices out of the box, held it with a
few napkins, and then left the kitchen.

"Where you going?" Sal asked.

Mickey didn't answer. As he headed down the stairs, he
heard his father's muffled voice screaming something at
him.

MICKEY GOT IN his car and went to talk to Artie in Artie's
"office," a bookie joint above a shoe store on Kings Highway
and East Sixteenth. Mickey only went there once in a while,
to see Artie, or on Friday and Saturday nights when the
OTB around the corner got too crowded.

As usual, there were about twenty guys packed into the
small room, filled with cigarette and cigar smoke. Bridge
tables with strewn *Racing Forms*, *Sports Eyes*, and betting
slips were set up all around the place, and Max, an old guy,
was taking bets at a table to the left. A TV attached to the
wall in the corner was showing odds from the Meadowlands, where, Mickey noticed, it was three minutes to post
time.

Mickey went up to Artie, who was sitting at a table in the
corner, bent over a *Sports Eye*. Artie had turned fifty last
year. He was short and bald, and he wore thick glasses. He
had a wife he sometimes talked about, but Mickey had
never met her or even seen her. Mickey sometimes won-

dered what any woman could possibly have in common with Artie, who seemed to spend all of his time at racetracks, bookie joints, and OTBs.

"Hey, Artie," Mickey said.

Artie didn't look up from the *Sports Eye*.

"You got my money?" Artie said.

"That's what I need to talk to you about," Mickey said.

"I don't want to talk about anything except money. What happened to your finger?"

"Cut it at work."

"Sorry to hear that. Where's my money?"

"Come on, Artie, just hear me out, will ya?"

"What's the matter?" Artie said. "It's not your money, it's this guy Angelo's, right?"

"Right."

"So what's the matter? He won't pay up?"

"I wouldn't say 'won't.'"

"Look," Artie said seriously. "I asked you if he could handle that kind of action and you said he could. I even let him put in another dime on the Rangers and now I expect to see that money."

"You don't understand," Mickey said.

"I don't want to understand," Artie said. "I made it very clear to you over the phone. I said, 'Angelo has this kind of money?' and you said, 'Yes.' That's all I heard and that's all I wanna hear now. He has to come up with the money and that's it."

"I asked Angelo for the money yesterday, and he said he'll pay it when he feels like it."

"That's not my problem."

"I know. I was just wondering if you had some advice for me."

"Advice? My advice is don't put in action for guys who can't pay. That's my advice."

Mickey was upset that Artie wasn't helping him, but he understood too. Artie wasn't a bookie himself; he was just a runner for Nick. Mickey couldn't expect him to put his job on the line.

"What race is going off here?" Mickey asked.

"The third."

"Like anything?"

"You're kiddin' me? You're in the hole for over a g, and you're gonna bet?"

"I'm not in the hole, Angelo is."

"Same difference."

"I'm just gonna throw away a few bucks. Who do you like?"

"The six, maybe the four. It's the fucking Meadowlands. It's like spinning a roulette wheel. Put a blindfold on and pin the tail on the fucking donkey."

"I'm gonna go put something in," Mickey said.

Mickey went up to the counter and played a ten-dollar exacta six-four, and played a four-six exacta for five dollars. Max wrote down Mickey's bets on a little piece of paper then gave Mickey the original and kept the carbon. In the back of his mind, Mickey was hoping he could win back Angelo's money.

When Mickey returned to the table, Artie said, "This race is a crap shoot. I think I'll just sit it out."

"Let me explain what's going on," Mickey said, almost whispering. "See, this guy Angelo—he's connected."

"So?"

"So that's why I put in the action for him."

"You're talkin' to a brick wall," Artie said. "I asked you on the phone about this guy, and you vouched for him."

"I know, it's my fault," Mickey said. "But what am I supposed to do?"

"Am I talking to myself here? If you want to close your account, I'll close your account. We can make up a payment plan, and when the account is paid off, you can start from scratch again."

"You think I should pay it off?"

"You said you got money in the bank, right?"

"That's my life savings so I can go to college next year. There's no way in hell I'm using that to pay off some stupid bets."

An old guy across the table glared at Mickey over a torn-out racing page from the *Daily News*.

"Keep your voice down—Jesus," Artie said. "You sound like my fucking wife for Chrissakes."

"Sorry," Mickey said.

"What do you want me to tell you?" Artie said.

Mickey glanced at the TV and saw the race had started. The four was on the lead—the six was on the rail, in behind horses. Mickey continued to watch the race as he said, "I'm not stupid, Artie. I don't just go around putting in action for guys I don't know. But this guy, Angelo, asked me to make the bets, and I couldn't say no to him."

"All the more reason why you should make a payment plan or just pay it out of your own pocket and start saving again," Artie said. "You asked for my advice and I gave it to you. Chalk it up to experience. What do you got here?"

"Four-six."

"Rip up your ticket. The six is dead as Kelso's nuts."

Mickey looked up and saw that the six horse was backing out of the picture.

"Hey, don't think I don't wanna help you out," Artie said. "Believe me, if there was anything I could do for you, I would, but Nick calls all the shots. Meanwhile, I'm up shit's creek with my own problems. I can't catch a cold at the races since—I don't remember the last time I cashed a fuckin' ticket. I got my own debts and bills. I'd be better off sitting on the couch watching TV with my fuckin' wife, but like an idiot I come here every night. How's your father by the way?"

"All right," Mickey said.

"He can't make it out to the track no more, huh?"

"Nah, those days are over," Mickey said. The race at the Meadowlands had ended. The four and six had finished last and next to last.

"I got a friend whose father had that Alzheimer's shit," Artie said. "It's hard. I give you a lot of credit for what you do—taking care of him like that. I know I never would've been able to baby-sit my old man."

"I better get going," Mickey said.

As Mickey stood up, Artie said, "I'll tell you what. I'll buy some time for you. I'll make up some story—your father's sick, was in the hospital, whatever. But all I can promise you is another few days. After that, I don't know what I can do. A thousand and change is a big fuckin' number—you'll have to start paying it off somehow. If you have to take it out of your own pocket, then you have to take it out of your own pocket. That's the best I can do for you."

"Thanks," Mickey said, leaning over and patting Artie on the back. "I owe you one."

AT THE NEWSSTAND under the Kings Highway subway el, Mickey bought a copy of *Sports Eye,* then he went to the OTB on East Sixteenth. Although Mickey only knew the names of a few people at the OTB, he knew almost all of their faces. He had been seeing the same people, hanging out at OTBs and racetracks, for most of his life.

The Sixteenth Street OTB was small—the whole place was about five hundred square feet—and you could see the cigarette smoke under the fluorescent lights. It was one of the only OTBs in Brooklyn that was open nights for the trotters at Roosevelt and Yonkers, and degenerates from the entire borough jammed into the place. It was so crowded, sometimes you couldn't get up to the windows in time to bet, and the spillover usually hung out on the sidewalk, pissing between cars and drinking beer out of paper bags.

When Mickey arrived, the usual crowd of dirty, tired-looking men were standing on the street in front of the OTB, smoking and reading their racing programs and scratch sheets. Mickey pushed and weaved his way through the loud, angry crowd, glancing up at one of the TV monitors. The fifth race at Yonkers was going off in seven minutes. There was a long line of people waiting to bet, so Mickey got a betting slip and stood at the end of the line while he used his copy of *Sports Eye* to handicap the race. It was very crowded and, on a normal night, Mickey would have headed back over to the bookie joint. But Artie was there and Mickey didn't want Artie to see him making more bets.

Mickey got his bet in seconds before the pool closed, then he made his way back toward the TV screen.

"Hey, who you got here?"

Mickey looked over and saw the guy with the gray hair and the bushy gray mustache. Although they talked just about every time they saw each other, Mickey wasn't sure what the guy's name was. A couple of years ago the guy had introduced himself to Mickey, and Mickey thought his name was Ray or Roy.

"The F," Mickey said.

OTB used letters to correspond with the numbers at the track, so the *F* was the six.

"He's missing a week," the guy said.

"He should get a good trip, though," Mickey said.

"I went with the D horse."

"Got as good a shot as any," Mickey said.

"I was by Yonkers last night," the guy went on. "Had the three in the last, needed it to get home the double. The three takes over at the top of the stretch, then the two comes out of the clouds to nail me. Can you believe that? The double comes back two and change—woulda been bigger if the three got it."

Mickey was shaking his head, as if he felt sorry for the guy, but the truth was he didn't give a shit.

As the horses were lining up behind the starting gate, Mickey looked around to see who else was in the OTB. He spotted the skinny Indian guy who bet the eight horse in every race. If the eight horse wasn't in contention, he would just stand there, not making a sound. But if the eight left the gate strong or started closing on the outside, he would start screaming like a madman: "Come on freight train, come on freight train!" The retarded guy with the red hair was standing in the corner, mumbling to himself as usual, and standing near the door was the father with his two kids. The kids—a girl and a boy—looked like they were about ten years old, and they always stood around, looking bored and lonely, while their father gambled.

Staring at the family, Mickey had missed the beginning of the race. It didn't matter because his six horse hadn't left the gate and the horse was sitting three deep on the rail. The six never made a move, and the four horse won the race easily.

"What'd I tell you?" the guy with the gray hair said to Mickey. "This is an easy fucking game. I shoulda put more on it. The horse was a fuckin' lock."

Mickey ripped up his losing ticket into tiny pieces, then he tossed the pieces onto the floor like confetti. He realized he was kidding himself, gambling tonight, chasing Angelo's money. He was about to go home when he imagined what it would be like—fighting with his father, or lying in bed with nothing to do, watching *The Odd Couple* and *The Honey-*

mooners for the zillionth time—and he decided to hang out for a few more races, see if he could make something happen.

Mickey was standing outside the OTB, reading *Sports Eye,* when he heard someone shout, "Hey, loser!"

Mickey looked toward the street and saw Chris smiling, sitting double-parked in his mother's Chevy. He was wearing a shiny electric blue satin jacket with the top four buttons undone and a gold link chain hanging in his chest hair. His hair was slicked back, and he had a lightning bolt earring in his left ear.

Chris said, "I knew I'd find you here, you fuckin' degenerate."

Mickey went over to talk to Chris. It smelled like he'd used an entire bottle of Paco Rabanne cologne.

"What're you doing here?" Mickey asked.

"I just had to do some shopping for my mother and I was passing by," Chris said. "So you winning any money at least?"

"Not tonight," Mickey said.

"What happened to your hand?"

"Oh, nothing," Mickey said. "Just a little accident at work."

"Yeah, right, probably jerking off too much," Chris said. "At least it's your right hand so you can still bowl. Hey, come out to the city tonight."

"The city?" Mickey said.

"Come on, I'm gonna hit a few bars, see if I can fuck a horny city chick. Maybe you can do her friend."

"Nah, I don't think so. Not tonight."

"Why? What're you gonna do, hang out with the old men on a Friday night?"

"I have to get up early tomorrow."

"What for?"

"Just to do some stuff around the house."

"Come on, come to the city with me," Chris said. "It'll do you good."

Mickey was looking back toward the OTB. The guy and his two sad-looking kids were hanging out in front surrounded by people screaming.

"All right," Mickey said to Chris. "What the fuck?"

MICKEY DROVE HOME and changed into a pair of dark green corduroys and a red button-down shirt. When Chris honked, Mickey went outside.

"What's with the outfit?" Chris said when Mickey got into the car. "You going to church or you going out drinking?"

"Fuck you," Mickey said.

"I'm just bustin' chops, man," Chris said. "You look great. The chicks are gonna be all over you tonight. Trust me, tonight's the night Mickey Prada finally gets laid."

4

DRIVING DOWN CONEY Island Avenue with one hand on the steering wheel, Chris said, "Me and Filippo saw *Debbie Does Dallas* the other night, what a great fuckin' movie, man. You know what's funny? It takes place in Brooklyn. You'd think with the title *Debbie Does Dallas,* it would be Dallas, but it's all Brooklyn. They got this one scene, an orgy, was shot in the locker room at Brooklyn College. Imagine you're going to school there, just walking by, and you see this orgy goin' on, what would you do? I know what I'd do. I'd have my pants down to my ankles, and I'd get three chicks on me at once. Man, what a great fuckin' movie that was."

"So where we going, anyway?" Mickey asked.

"New bar on Twenty-third called Live Bait," Chris said. "Guy at work told me about it. He said soap opera stars hang out there. Maybe we'll meet Genie Francis."

"Can't we go someplace else?" Mickey said. "How about one of those Irish pubs up on Second Avenue?"

"Irish pub?" Chris said. "What do you want to do, fuck an old man?"

"You know what I mean," Mickey said. "Someplace more laid-back."

"Just sit back and relax," Chris said. "Uncle Chris'll take care of the entertainment this evening."

They continued around the traffic circle near the Parade Grounds, heading toward the entrance to the Prospect Expressway. Chris turned up the volume on the radio, blasting "Back in Black."

When the song ended, Chris turned the volume back down and said, "You watch wrestling last week?"

"Nah," Mickey said, staring out the window.

"You don't know what you missed, man," Chris said. "They had George 'The Animal' Steele on. He comes out with all this spit dribbling out of his mouth, then he starts chewing up the ring. I'm serious. He was eating the ropes and the posts, and they show all this cotton and rubber and shit, coming out of his mouth. You shoulda been there. I was laughin' my fuckin' ass off."

Mickey was thinking about the girl from the fish store, remembering her green eyes and that great smile.

"Hey, douche bag," Chris said. "Douche bag."

"Yeah?" Mickey said, snapping out of it.

"What's wrong with you? Why're you zoning out? You start smokin' weed or something?"

"I was just thinking," Mickey said.

"What're you thinking about, horses?"

Chris laughed.

"I wasn't thinking about anything," Mickey said. He was suddenly angry and he didn't know why.

"Hey, I was gonna ask you," Chris said, "what's going on with you and that Mafia man?"

"Mafia man?" Mickey said, pretending to forget. "Oh, *him*. That's all taken care of."

"He gave you the money?"

"Yeah, he gave me the money."

"See?" Chris said. "You were shittin' bricks for nothing."

They took the Brooklyn Battery Tunnel into the city. Although East Flatbush, Mickey's neighborhood, was only about eight miles from Manhattan, it might as well have been on a different continent. Hardly anybody in his neighborhood went into the city, unless they worked there or had some other reason to visit.

Driving up Broadway through Soho, Chris said, "You believe people live in these old fucking buildings? They don't even got walls, and you can see all the pipes in the ceiling."

A few minutes later, driving through the Village, Chris started making fun of the kids with spiky green hair and mohawks.

"Look at that one. He looks like a fuckin' Indian. Can you believe people *pay* to look like that?"

They drove up to Twenty-third Street and found a parking space around the corner from the bar. They were only a few blocks away from Baruch College, where Mickey had been supposed to start school this year.

"You sure you wanna go in here?" Mickey said to Chris, while they were waiting on line to be proofed.

"What's wrong with it?" Chris said.

"It looks too uptight," Mickey said.

"What are you talkin' about? Wait till you see the hot fuckin' chicks in this place. And they don't pussy around, either. These city chicks come to play, you know what I mean? I wish I had some coke on me."

"Why?" Mickey asked.

"You know what they say," Chris said, "blow for blow. You give these chicks some coke, they'll take you back into the bathroom and suck the rust off your tailpipe."

The bouncer waved Chris in, but asked to see Mickey's driver's license. Chris had gotten Mickey a fake one last year, which made him nineteen. The bouncer looked at Mickey and at the license a couple of times before letting Mickey inside.

"Come on," Chris said to Mickey, smiling. "Let's get laid!"

The front bar area was jam-packed with rich-looking guys—some in suits and ties, others wearing Izods with the collars flipped up—and beautiful women in expensive clothes. Mickey felt very out of place. Chris, dressed like a guido, didn't fit in, either.

Chris weaved ahead of Mickey through the crowd, smiling at all the women he passed, and a few times he stopped and talked into their ears. Some song about turning Japanese was blaring, and Mickey couldn't hear what Chris was saying, but none of the girls stopped and some of them made disgusted faces while they walked away.

At the bar, Chris bought Mickey a Bud and a shot of something green.

"What is it?" Mickey asked.

"Just suck it down," Chris said.

Mickey did the shot, wincing as if it were poison, then chased it with some beer.

"Come on, smile," Chris said. "If you stand around, looking like a fuckin' sourpuss, girls'll never look at you." Chris started smiling. "See that blonde over there? The one with the big knockers and the nice caboose?"

Mickey looked over. The girl had straight shoulder-length hair, and she looked like she had probably grown up in the city in some fancy apartment uptown, maybe on Park Avenue. She was with another girl who looked the same except her hair was brown.

"Yeah, what about her?" Mickey asked.

"Look how fuckin' hot she is," Chris said. "She has the big blow-job lips and the blonde hair just like Bambi Woods."

"Who?" Mickey said.

"Debbie," Chris said. "Come on, you get the friend."

"Hold up," Mickey said.

"What's wrong?"

"Don't you think those girls are out of our league?"

"What do you mean?"

"They're not gonna wanna talk to us."

"How do you know?"

"Because I can tell. They're looking for some Wall Street guys with money, that's why they came to this place."

"Watch the doctor operate," Chris said.

Mickey shook his head and followed Chris over to the two girls. Chris started talking to the blonde. The other girl looked at Mickey, then she whispered something to her friend and walked away.

Chris continued to talk to the blonde. Mickey felt stupid, standing by himself, so he went back to the bar and finished his Bud. After a few minutes, Chris returned.

"Fuckin' skanky city bitch," Chris said.

"What happened?" Mickey asked.

"I was talking to her, getting her to laugh and shit, then she tells me she's 'with somebody tonight.' I knew she was full of shit, feeding me a line, but I didn't feel like playing that game, you know? It's not like she's the last chick on the fuckin' planet . . . What happened with your chick?"

"We have a date Saturday night," Mickey said.

"You know what your problem is?" Chris said. "It's your attitude, that's what your problem is."

"My attitude?"

"Yeah."

"The girl walked away from me."

"But why'd she walk away? That's the question you gotta ask yourself. Maybe if you said something to her or even smiled, she would've stuck around. You can't just look at a girl like you hate the world and expect to get laid."

Chris took out a pack of cigarettes from his jacket pocket and jutted one toward Mickey.

"No thanks," Mickey said.

"That's another problem," Chris said, "when you go to a bar you gotta smoke. Chicks like guys who smoke. Besides, if you got some smoke into your clothes, you wouldn't smell like the freakin' Fulton Fish Market."

"Fuck you," Mickey said.

Chris laughed. "Come on, Mick, you're my friend and shit, but everybody knows you smell like Charlie the fuckin' Tuna."

"Work at a fish store—see how you smell at the end of the day."

"Can't you at least shower?"

"Fuck you."

"I'm trying to be your friend," Chris said, "but you gotta do something because no girl's gonna wanna talk to you when you smell like you've been cleaning fish tanks."

"Come on, let's just get out of here," Mickey said. "We'll go to a diner or something."

"Why, you want some coffee and cake, Grandma?"

Chris ordered another beer and another shot. Mickey stood around, drinking water, as Chris drank beer after beer and got blown off by girl after girl. Each time a girl rejected Chris, he seemed even more pissed off.

About an hour had gone by since Mickey had stopped drinking when he said, "So you ready to throw in the towel?"

"What about her?"

Mickey looked to his right where Chris was looking and saw a thin girl with dirty blonde hair standing next to a girl with short red hair. Two guys in sharp black suits were talking to them.

"I think they're taken," Mickey said.

"Fuck taken," Chris said, obviously shit-faced. "Those guys just came over to them. I like the blonde—she's got that slutty, Madonna thing going on. Hello, sweetheart. Look this way. Fuck this, watch my beer."

Chris stumbled up to the two girls. Chris said something to the blonde, and the blonde turned away. Suddenly, Chris looked angry. He grabbed the blonde's arm. She tried to get free, but Chris wouldn't let go. The two guys in suits tried to pull Chris off the girl, then Chris started going after the two guys. Chris connected with a couple of punches, and one of the guys punched Chris in the face. The bouncer came over and pulled Chris away. Chris was still cursing and screaming as the bouncer pushed him out of the bar.

Mickey went outside. The bouncer had Chris against a wall and was talking to him. Chris's face was red and he was still screaming. The skin below Chris's right eye was bright pink, and blood was dripping from his lips.

Finally, the bouncer returned to the bar, and Mickey went over to Chris.

"Nice going," Mickey said.

Chris's hair was a mess and he was sweating.

"Come on," Mickey said, "let's just get the fuck out of here."

"No way," Chris said. "I said I'm getting you laid—and I'm getting you laid."

Mickey followed Chris to the car, trying to talk him into going back to Brooklyn, but Chris wouldn't listen.

When they got to the car, Mickey said, "Lemme drive."

"No way," Chris said. "You drive like a woman."

"There's no way I'm getting in the car with you," Mickey said. "You must've had six beers and all those shots."

"Then take the subway home. I don't give a shit."

Mickey thought about it, but a white guy taking the subway back to Brooklyn at one in the morning was like a death sentence.

"Come on, just give me the keys," Mickey said.

"Get in or I'm goin' alone," Chris said.

Mickey stood on the curb.

"Okay," Chris said, and he started to pull away up Twenty-third Street. Mickey ran after the car, banging on the passenger-side door. Chris stopped and Mickey got in.

"This is bullshit," Mickey said. "I'm never going out with you again."

"Ooh, you're hurting me," Chris said, laughing.

"Slow down," Mickey said.

"You kiddin'? They call me Mario-fuckin'-Andretti. Check this shit out."

Chris stepped hard on the gas pedal, right as the light was turning red, barely beating the traffic on Fifth Avenue. Laughing, Chris zigzagged by a taxi. The driver of the cab stuck out his middle finger, and Chris swerved in front of the cab and hit the brake suddenly. The cabdriver braked too to avoid smashing into Chris's car.

"What the fuck's wrong with you?" Mickey said.

Chris turned off the engine, then he got out of the car and went back to the cab, taking the car keys with him. Mickey watched Chris and the driver yell at each other, then the driver got out of the cab and Chris started fighting with him in the middle of Twenty-third Street. The driver, who looked Pakistani or Indian, tried to punch Chris and missed, then Chris pushed him back against the cab and started punching and kicking him. The driver fell to his knees, his turban unraveling onto the street, but Chris wouldn't let up, kicking him in the face until blood started gushing from his nose.

A few other cars had stopped, and some people were standing around, watching. Finally, Chris stopped beating up the driver and got back into the car with Mickey.

"Give me the car keys," Mickey said.

"Move over," Chris said.

"No," Mickey said.

"You got two choices," Chris said, "move over or get the fuck out."

"Asshole," Mickey said and slid over. Chris turned on the engine and sped away.

"Shit," Chris said, looking down at his legs. "That scumbag got blood on my jeans."

"Watch the road," Mickey said.

"I'm watching, I'm watching," Chris said.

"You're such an idiot," Mickey said. "You forget you have a police record? If the cops catch you fighting with bouncers and cabbies, they're gonna put you in jail. No juvie this time—real jail."

"The guy gave me the finger."

"So?"

"See? That's your problem, Prada. You let people step all over you. You gotta learn to do the stepping yourself for a change."

Chris ran a red on Seventh.

"Where the fuck are we going, anyway?" Mickey said.

"To get you laid. Where else?"

Now Mickey realized what Chris had in mind.

"No way," Mickey said.

"Too late," Chris said.

"Come on, just pull over."

"Nope."

Chris continued speeding down Twenty-third Street, swinging a sharp right onto Tenth Avenue.

"You're a real dick, you know that?" Mickey said.

"Gee, and I thought I was doin' you a favor," Chris said, "finally gettin' you some."

"I don't want to go to a whore, all right?"

"So what're you gonna do? Stay a virgin the rest of your life?"

"What makes you think I'm a virgin?"

Chris gave Mickey a look then said, "Come on, who did you fuck, Linda Gianetti? You told me nothing happened with her."

Mickey remembered his date with Linda in tenth grade. He took her to see *ET* and near the part at the end, where ET phones home, he put his hand on her leg. When the movie ended, Linda said she was tired and wanted to go home and she never wanted to go out with him again.

"Maybe I lied," Mickey said.

"Yeah, right," Chris said. "No guy in the world would ever lie about getting laid. Guys only lie about *not* getting laid."

Chris turned left onto Twenty-seventh Street, past some barren factory buildings.

"Can you please pull over and let me drive?" Mickey said.

"No way," Chris said. "Not till you meet Betty."

"Who's Betty?"

"*That's* Betty."

Screeching the brakes, Chris pulled over to the curb and parked. A tall black woman in a leopard-skin brassiere and a short black leather skirt wobbled toward the car on what looked like four-inch pumps.

Chris got out of the car and went around to talk to Betty.

Mickey watched Chris go into his wallet and hand Betty some bills. Betty looked drugged out, or drunk, the way she was trying to balance herself. Still, Mickey couldn't help feeling turned on. She had a sexy body—big high breasts, long legs—and her face was surprisingly attractive for a hooker—smooth skin, lips painted with bright red lipstick.

Chris returned to the car and said to Mickey, "Happy fucking," then he walked away and Betty opened the driver-side door and said to Mickey, "Wanna move to the back, baby?"

Mickey knew he would never live it down with Chris if he didn't go through with this. Besides, Betty looked good.

Mickey lifted the button on the back door, and then he stood out of the car. Betty got in the back. Before Mickey got in with her, he looked over at Chris, standing several yards away. Chris was smiling, sticking his index finger in and out of his partially closed fist.

The backseat of Chris's car was covered with newspaper, soda cans, and other junk. Mickey swatted away as much of the garbage as he could onto the floor, then he sat down next to Betty and closed the door.

"Something smells *nasty* in here," Betty said, making a face.

Mickey didn't smell anything unusual except for Betty's strong perfume.

"It's probably just the car," Mickey said. "My friend's kind of a slob."

"It ain't the car," Betty said, "it's you. You smell like fish."

"Oh, that's just because I work in a fish store," Mickey

said, thinking there couldn't be anything more humiliating than a cheap hooker telling him he smelled.

"Your body clean?" Betty asked.

"Yeah," Mickey said. "Of course."

"We'll see. Take down your pants so I can suck on your dick."

Mickey pulled down his pants to his ankles. His heart was racing and he was starting to sweat.

"Your friend say it's your first time," Betty said.

"It's not my first time," Mickey said confidently.

"Whatever, don't matter to me none."

Betty's cold dry hand reached under Mickey's underwear. It felt weird but good, having someone else touching his dick. Mickey didn't know what he was supposed to do next, if he was supposed to touch her back. He started running his fingers through her greasy hair, but this didn't seem right, so he put his hand on her leg instead.

"Feels like you ready for me," Betty said.

She pulled up her skirt then grabbed Mickey's hand and moved it up her thigh. It was dark in the car—the only light came from the lampposts outside. Mickey closed his eyes, the idea slowly coming to him that something was wrong.

Mickey jerked his hand away and jumped off the seat, banging his head against the roof of the car on the way out.

"What's the matter?" Betty said.

Suddenly, her voice sounded deeper, more manly.

Mickey pulled on his underwear and pants and got out of the car as fast as he could. Chris was standing on the sidewalk, laughing hysterically.

"Party on, boys," Betty said to Chris as he walked away, swinging his butt.

Chris, still laughing, was keeled far over, his head almost against his knees.

Mickey, his face bright pink, said, "Gimme the fuckin' car keys, you asshole."

5

WHEN VINCENT'S FISH market opened for business at ten A.M. on Saturday, Mickey was hoping Harry would leave for the day, but Charlie hadn't shown up yet, so Harry had to stick around. At around ten-thirty, Harry called Charlie at home but there was no answer.

"He better have a good excuse or I'm gonna fire him," Harry said.

Around lunchtime, Mickey was hoping Angelo would show up to finally square his debt. The last time Mickey had seen Angelo was last Tuesday, and he was starting to wonder if he would ever see him again.

Harry called Charlie a few more times, but by one-thirty there was still no answer. Mickey hadn't taken a break all day, and he was exhausted. Afraid he'd slip with the knife and cut himself again, he went to the deli up the block and bought a pastrami-on-rye and a cup of coffee.

When Mickey returned to the fish store, Charlie was

standing near the cash register. The lower part of Charlie's left arm was in a cast, and he had bruises on his face.

"Jesus, what happened?" Mickey asked.

"He's in the middle of telling me the story," Harry said. Then he said to Charlie, "So did you see what they looked like?"

"A few of 'em," Charlie said, "but it don't make a difference. The cops said they'll look for them, but I know that's just bullshit. The cops don't give a shit what happens to two black dudes. But if we was white and the other guys was black, they'd have 'em arrested overnight—guaranteed."

"Hey, I know I told you this before," Harry said, "but you never listen to me. You gotta be careful about where you go at night. You gotta stay out of the white neighborhoods." Harry took off his apron. "Anyway, I'm glad to see you're alive, and now I can leave to go to my dentist appointment I had three hours ago. By the way, you're only getting a half day's pay today."

"*What?*" Charlie said. "You can see what happened to me, can't you?"

"Yes, and I'm very sorry," Harry said, "but it's no excuse for not calling in. You have my home number—you could've called me this morning."

"Ah, come on, man," Charlie said.

"So long," Harry said, smiling as he left the store.

"Motherfucker," Charlie said. "If I had to get my arm fuckin' cut off, he'd try to dock me. Son of a bitch piece of shit."

"What happened?" Mickey asked.

"You heard him? 'You gotta stay out of the white neigh-borhoods at night.' Like it's my fault 'cause I'm black? Like I gotta sit home all night in my house like I got a curfew. Fuck him, man."

"Come on, tell me," Mickey said.

Charlie let out a deep breath then said, "My cousin was DJ'in' this sweet sixteen party in Mill Basin last night. I wanna start gettin' into DJ'in' myself, you know, so I went with him. Anyway, we was leaving, standing outside the house, when Jerome, my cousin, starts talkin' to this white girl. Then these white dudes come out and start saying shit, calling us niggers and shit. My cousin started saying shit back to them, then one of the white dudes goes away and comes out with one of them aluminum baseball bats. My cousin and me, we run, trying to get to our car. But the dude's behind us, swinging the bat. He got my arm, but I made it inside. But they had Jerome up against the car out-side. The dude was swinging the bat at him, and I was in the car, watching. What the fuck was I supposed to do? I thought if I opened the door the guys would drag me out and beat me too. So I just started honking on the horn, and then these other people came over and the guys just ran. Jerome was in bad shape, man. Lost a lot of blood, broke bones and shit everywhere, but they got him in stable con-dition now. It's gonna be in the paper—somebody from the *Post* talked to us at the hospital last night."

"Jesus," Mickey said.

"Whatever," Charlie said. "I just feel bad 'cause I didn't do nothing. I was just sittin' there in the car, watchin' it hap-pen."

"You did the right thing," Mickey said. "If you got out they could've killed you."

"Or maybe I could've saved my cousin's ass."

"Or maybe you *did* save his ass," Mickey said. "Maybe if you didn't honk on the horn, no one would've come over and scared the guys off. Maybe if you went out there, you both would've been killed."

"Yeah, maybe you're right," Charlie said, "but I still feel like I did him wrong."

"Can I get you something?" Mickey asked. "You want something to drink? You want some of my sandwich?"

"That's all right," Charlie said. "I just wanna forget about it. That's why I came into work today. So I could go on with my life, you know? I ain't gonna let those motherfuckers keep me at home."

Mickey took a bite of his sandwich and washed it down with a gulp of coffee. He took another bite when the bell above the door rang, and the girl who had been in the fish store yesterday walked in. She was wearing a lot of makeup today, especially around her eyes, and she must have done something with her hair because it looked fuller and bigger than Mickey remembered. Her legs looked perfect, in tight purple acid-washed jeans, and she was wearing a baggy white sweater.

"Remember me?" the girl asked.

Mickey didn't know what to say or do. He just stood there, staring. He remembered he had a bite of food in his mouth and swallowed it, then he said, "Sure I remember you. Hey, I'm really sorry about yesterday. My boss is just an asshole sometimes."

"Amen," Charlie said.

"What happened to *you?*" the girl asked Charlie.

"Nothing," Charlie said, "just fell off my bike last night." Then he said to Mickey, "I gotta go wash up," and he exited to the back of the store.

"So can I get you something?" Mickey asked the girl.

"No, thank you," the girl said. "Actually, I just came by to see how you were doing."

"You did?" Mickey said.

"Yeah," the girl said. "I felt bad for leaving yesterday, but someone was waiting in the car for me and I didn't want to buy anything from your boss. So how's your finger?"

"It's fine, see?" Mickey said, holding up his bandaged hand.

"Well, I'm glad."

"Don't you want something?" Mickey asked. "The fluke and flounder are fresh today. Also the kingfish is really nice."

"No, I'm sorry. Maybe some other time. Anyway, I'm glad you're feeling better. See you around."

"Bye," Mickey said.

Mickey watched the girl leave the store. Charlie returned from the back and said, "Where'd she go?"

"She left," Mickey said.

"You get the digits?" Charlie asked.

"Nah," Mickey said.

"What you talkin' 'bout, Willis?" Charlie said. "Can't you tell that girl was in heat?"

"It's not like that," Mickey said. "She just came here to see how I was feeling."

Charlie stared at Mickey, his hands crossed in front of his chest.

Mickey stood there for several seconds longer, then he went around the fish stands and dashed out the door. He looked both ways, up and down Flatbush Avenue, but he didn't see the girl anywhere. He was about to go back into the fish store when he spotted her coming out of the video store across the street. Mickey darted into traffic, not seeing the station wagon speeding right toward him. The driver of the station wagon slammed on the brakes, and the car screeched to a stop, inches in front of Mickey.

"Fuckin' moron!" the driver shouted, leaning out of the window.

Continuing across the street, Mickey didn't see a motorcycle coming from the other direction. The motorcycle sped past Mickey, barely missing him. Mickey waited in traffic for two more cars to pass, then he sprinted toward the sidewalk where the girl was staring at him, with her mouth partway open.

"Are you all right?" she asked.

"Yeah," Mickey said, catching his breath. "I'm fine."

"You almost got killed."

"I know, I'm sorry. I just saw you and I was afraid you'd get into a car or something and drive away."

Mickey stared at the girl. He noticed she was wearing the same great perfume she had worn yesterday.

"Do you want to go to dinner or a movie sometime?" Mickey asked. "If you don't want to that's okay too. I mean I—"

"I'd love to," the girl said.

"You would?" Mickey said. "I mean that's great. So do you have a phone?"

"Do I have a *phone?*"

"I mean phone number."

"Do you have a piece of paper?"

"No, but if you tell me I'll remember it."

The girl told Mickey her phone number then said, "But how will I know it's you when you call?"

"Sorry, I'm Mickey."

The girl sang, *"Oh Mickey, you're so fine, you're so fine you blow my mind, hey Mickey."*

Mickey smiled then said, "Who do I ask for when I call?"

"Rhonda."

"Rhonda," he said. "Great."

They both laughed nervously. Mickey noticed the way Rhonda's teeth weren't perfect—the two front ones stuck out a little too far and overlapped slightly—but it was still the best-looking smile he'd ever seen.

Mickey realized he was staring at her again and said, "So I'll definitely call you soon."

"Okay," Rhonda said. "Bye."

Mickey watched Rhonda walk away, liking how her thighs rubbed together in her tight jeans. When she reached the end of the block, she looked back at Mickey and smiled, then she turned the corner and was gone.

When Mickey returned to the fish store, his face glowing, Charlie said, "See? Now ain't you glad I came in to work today?"

ON SUNDAY, MICKEY'S day off, he woke up around ten and cooked bacon and eggs, leaving some extra in the pan for his father, who was still sleeping. After breakfast, Mickey watched some of *Davey and Goliath,* then he flipped through old *Sports Illustrated*s until the Jets-Colts game came on at one o'clock.

During halftime of the four o'clock game—the Giants-Buccaneers—Mickey took a walk to Rocco's Pizzeria on Avenue J and picked up a pepperoni pie for dinner. When he returned to his apartment, he heard his father screaming from inside the bathroom.

"What's going on?" Mickey said from the hallway. "What's wrong?"

"Get me outta here!" Sal screamed. "Get me the fuck outta here!"

"Just unlock the door," Mickey said, trying to twist the handle.

"You locked me in here, you son of a bitch," Sal said. "I'm gonna kill you!"

Sal started banging against the door. Then someone started knocking on the door to the stairwell.

It was Joseph, the landlord who lived in the apartment downstairs.

"It's all right!" Mickey yelled. "It's just my father!"

"Will you shut him the fuck up?" Joseph yelled back. "It's Sunday for Chrissakes!"

Sal was still screaming and cursing, banging frantically on the bathroom door. Blackie, Joseph's German shepherd, was barking furiously in the apartment downstairs.

"Stand back," Mickey said.

Sal was still screaming and banging.

"I said stand back!"

Finally, it was quiet for a few moments, then Mickey rammed against the door, shoulder first, but the door didn't open.

"Hey, what the hell are you doing?" Joseph yelled from the stairwell.

Mickey rammed against the door again and again, and on his fourth try, the lock gave way and the door swung open.

Sal was standing huddled in the corner near the toilet bowl, looking terrified.

"It's all right, Dad," Mickey said. "It's okay."

Mickey took a step forward, reaching out to touch his father, when Sal suddenly pushed by him, almost knocking him into the shower stall.

"What the fuck's wrong with you?" Mickey said as Sal went down the hallway into the bedroom and slammed the door.

Later, Joseph installed a temporary hook lock on the bathroom door and told Mickey there would be a one-hundred-dollar surcharge on the rent next month to replace the original lock and repair the damage to the door.

Mickey spent the rest of the day alone in his room. After the Giants game, he picked up the phone and dialed the first six digits of Rhonda's number, then he hung up, deciding he was just wasting his time.

AROUND TWO O'CLOCK on Monday afternoon, Angelo Santoro strutted into Vincent's Fish Market. He was wearing a long black wool coat over a dark suit.

"How ya doin', kid?" Angelo said.

"Pretty good," Mickey said, hoping Angelo would take out his wallet.

Angelo noticed Charlie in the store and said, "What happened to you?"

"Fell off my bike," Charlie said.

"Sorry to hear that," Angelo said. Then he turned back to Mickey and said, "Can we talk in private? Maybe step outside or something?"

Mickey looked at Angelo's coat, not seeing any bulge where his gun might be. He grabbed his jacket and followed him out the door.

"Sorry I've been a little incognito lately," Angelo said to Mickey when they got outside. "I've just had a lot of business to take care of lately with my boss, you know? I hope you understand."

"I understand," Mickey said. "Of course I understand. I mean I knew it had to be something like that."

Angelo took out a pack of cigarettes from his coat pocket. "Smoke?"

"No thanks," Mickey said.

"Smart man. Probably save ten years on your life. Me? I'll probably never know my grandkids. It's all right, though. You gotta live life to love life, right?" Angelo lit his cigarette and took a long drag on it. After he blew smoke out of his mouth and nose, he said, "So you got the lines on tonight's game?"

Mickey smiled, hoping that Angelo was just joking. But by the way Angelo was looking at him, waiting for him to answer, Mickey knew he wasn't.

"I don't know what the lines are," Mickey said, not smiling anymore.

"It don't matter," Angelo said. "I'm gonna take it easy this week. Just put in two dollars on the Seahawks, will ya?"

"Two dollars" meant two hundred times, or another eleven hundred *real* dollars with the vig.

"I'm sorry," Mickey said, "but I can't do that. Not *can't*— it's just my bookie says I need the money from your other bets first."

"I know my figure," Angelo said, "and if you want to know the truth, that's pocket change for me. I take a junket to Vegas, I drop ten g's in a weekend. I never heard of a bookie don't give a guy a chance to get even on a thousand bucks."

"I know what you're saying," Mickey said. "I really do. Maybe if you just paid off your debt this one time, I could talk to my bookie and—"

"How come you didn't tell me this before I made my first bet?"

"What do you mean?"

"Why didn't you tell me your bookie makes you keep a low number?"

"I don't know," Mickey said. "I mean I—"

"Maybe if you told me, I wouldn't've wasted my time. I would've known if I bet any serious money, I wouldn't be able to get even. The way I look at this, this is your fault. So what do you think we should do about that?"

"I don't think it's my fault," Mickey said.

"So what're you saying? You saying you think it's *my* fault?"

"No," Mickey said, his face burning up. "I don't think it's anybody's fault. I think—"

"Call your bookie," Angelo said.

"I'd like to, Angelo, but—"

"Will you let me finish? Call your fuckin' bookie. If the bet loses, I'll be here tomorrow at noon to pay off my whole figure, clean the slate. If the bet wins, we'll roll it over to next week. Tell your bookie I want the line in the paper today—Seattle minus three and a half. He has a problem, tell him to call Angelo Santoro from the Colombo family. You think he'll have a problem with that?"

"I'm not putting your bet in," Mickey said.

Angelo stared at Mickey for a long time, maybe five seconds.

"Excuse me?" Angelo said.

"I said I'm not putting your bet in," Mickey said. "I shouldn't've put in your other bets, either."

"You know who the fuck you're talking to?" Angelo said.

"Yeah, I know who I'm talking to," Mickey said.

Angelo grinned. He looked both ways, seeing no one was around, then he punched Mickey in the gut. Mickey keeled over, wheezing, trying to breathe.

"Sorry, did that hurt?" Angelo said, then he punched Mickey again, harder. Angelo said something in Italian Mickey didn't understand, then he grabbed Mickey by his neck, under his chin, and lifted him up.

"You better watch what you say and who you say it to, unless you wanna wind up in pieces. You disrespect me, you disrespect my whole family, you got that? I said, you got that?"

Mickey couldn't get the breath to speak, so he just nodded.

"Good," Angelo said. He looked at his watch then said in a suddenly friendly voice, "I gotta run, kid. Root for the Seahawks tonight, will ya? Hey, and I didn't forget about those

Jets-Giants tickets, neither—I'll bring 'em for you tomorrow afternoon. You take it easy now."

Angelo walked calmly up the block and turned the corner.

Mickey straightened up slowly. He felt nauseous and the pain in his stomach wouldn't stop. Gradually, he could breathe again, but he wasn't ready to walk. He stood there, holding his stomach, for about a minute, then he went back into the fish store, cursing.

"What's wrong?" Charlie asked.

"Nothing," Mickey said. He went behind the counter and tried to get busy cleaning up with a wet rag, but his stomach hurt with every movement.

"Second ago you was all smiles," Charlie said, "now you actin' like somebody died. Who is that dude Angelo, anyway?"

"Nobody," Mickey mumbled.

"What's that?" Charlie asked.

"Just a guy I know," Mickey said louder.

"So what'd he want to talk to you about out there?"

"Nothing much," Mickey said, rubbing the countertop so hard his wrist hurt.

"He give you them Jets-Giants tickets yet?" Charlie asked.

"No," Mickey said, hoping Charlie would shut up.

"When you get those tickets, I hope you gonna take me with you. New York versus New York. That game's gonna be the joint, man."

Mickey brought a couple of pounds of flounder fillets home from work, but he wasn't hungry and he didn't feel like cooking for his father. He left the fish in the fridge then he got in his car and drove to Kings Highway. He found a spot at a meter and went up to the bookie joint.

"I hope you got my money," Artie said to Mickey.

"We gotta talk," Mickey said.

"That doesn't sound good."

"I'm serious," Mickey said.

"Look," Artie said. "I got you a few extra days, that was the best I could do. I'm sorry, no more extensions."

"I don't want an extension. Can't we go somewhere?"

"I just walked in."

"The hallway at least. Give me two minutes. Just two minutes, I promise."

Shaking his head, Artie followed Mickey out of the bookie joint. They went down the stairs, outside, and stood under the subway el, by the pizza place.

"You eat yet?" Mickey asked.

"I thought you wanted to talk," Artie said.

"But if you're hungry, I'll buy you a slice. Come on."

"Look, can you tell me what the fuck is going on?" Artie said. "And I don't want to hear that Angelo isn't paying up, because I warned you about that before he made his first bet."

"It's more complicated now," Mickey said.

"I'm going back upstairs—"

"Come on, listen to me. I'm in trouble now. Big trouble."

"Just get me some money," Artie said. "Five hundred bucks even. We can work on a payment plan for the rest."

"He wants me to put in more action for him."

"Forget about it—"

"Please, just hear me out."

"I don't care what you say, I'm not putting in any more action for you or Angelo till I start seeing some money."

"He said we don't have a choice."

"We? Who are we now, Fred and Ginger?"

"He said he's in the Colombo family."

"It's not very hard to pretend you're a wiseguy," Artie said. "You just gotta watch *The Godfather* a few times, and anybody can do it."

"I thought about that," Mickey said, "but it doesn't make sense. Why would someone just pretend to be in the mob?"

"Gee, I don't know," Artie said, "maybe to get some free football bets?"

"Yeah, but why would somebody go to all that trouble," Mickey said, "coming to the fish store every day, dressing up like a mob guy?"

"Okay, what's this 'Angelo's' last name?" Artie said. "I'll ask around, see if I can find out if he's for real or not."

"You don't have to do that," Mickey said.

"You don't know his last name, do you?"

"Of course I do—it's Santoro."

"Santoro? As in Salvadore Santoro?"

"Who?"

"Salvadore Santoro—Tom Mix. He's the underboss for the Lucchese family. Don't you read the papers?"

Now the name Santoro sounded vaguely familiar to Mickey.

"What does that have to do with anything?" Mickey asked.

"You ever think your friend Angelo might've lied to you about his name?"

"I guess it's possible."

"Possible?" Artie said, smiling. "Angelo told you he's with the *Colombo* family, not the Lucchese family."

"So?" Mickey said, "Maybe there're two Santoros in two different families."

"Face it," Artie said, "you got taken for a ride."

"Fuck you," Mickey said. "You don't know what you're talking about. Angelo Santoro could be in the mob. Why couldn't he be?"

"What're we talking about here, anyway?" Artie said. "You want to believe Angelo's in the mob, believe he's in the mob. I thought we were talking about my money?"

"Don't worry, you'll get your money."

"When, Ginger?"

"Put in this one more bet for me."

"No."

"Come on."

"Fuck you."

"I swear, this is the last time—"

"The answer is no—*NO*. I'm doing this for your own good, Mickey. You know what they say at the OTB—'Bet with your head, not over it.' Well, you're over your head. Way over it."

"How about you give me the number of another bookie?"

"Do yourself a favor," Artie said, "quit while you're behind. Put off school, get a part-time job, work nights, weekends, park cars, answer phones—do whatever you gotta do to straighten this thing out."

"Thanks," Mickey said, walking away.

"You got till Wednesday," Artie called after him. "And don't do nothing stupid. Whatever you do, don't put in any more action for this guy. I'm warning you—he's bad news."

DRIVING HOME ON Kings Highway, Mickey thought it through both ways. If he didn't put the bet in and the Seahawks lost, Angelo would still be in the hole to Artie for 1,020 bucks. If he put the bet in and the Seahawks won, Angelo would show up tomorrow, thinking his debt was knocked down to twenty bucks and Mickey would have to make up the thousand-dollar difference to Artie. Either way, Mickey would be fucked, so he decided he had to figure out some way to put in Angelo's bet. At least then there was a chance Angelo could almost break even.

Mickey pulled over at a phone booth and called Nick, Artie's boss.

"Hey, Nick, it's Mickey . . . Mickey Prada. You know, Artie's friend."

Mickey hardly knew Nick, and Nick waited a few seconds before he said, "Yeah, right."

"Sorry to call you, but I couldn't find Artie by Kings Highway, and I wanted to put a bet in on the football game tonight."

"What do you want?" Nick asked.

"It's not me, it's my friend Angelo. He wants two hundred times Seahawks."

"Angelo?" Nick said. "Isn't that the guy Artie said's still shy?"

"Yeah, but Angelo squared that this afternoon," Mickey said. "I got the money with me in my pocket, right now."

"*All* of it?" Nick said.

"Yeah, all of it," Mickey said.

"Okay, if you say so," Nick said.

When Mickey opened the front door to his apartment, he smelled cooked fish. He went into the kitchen and saw Sal Prada sitting at the table, eating sautéed flounder and a bowl of spaghetti with tomato sauce, reading a newspaper.

"You cooked by yourself," Mickey said, surprised.

"Of course I cooked," Sal said. "Why can't I cook? There's more on the stove if you want some."

Mickey made a plate of spaghetti and fish and ate across from his father at the little two-seat Formica table. They didn't talk, but at least they weren't fighting.

After dinner, Mickey went into his room to watch the football game. Mickey rooted for the Seahawks, but it didn't help. Although they beat the Raiders 17–14, they were laying three and a half points, so Angelo lost his bet by one half point. Now the debt to Artie and Nick was $2,120, and Mickey was suddenly positive he would never see Angelo Santoro again.

6

MICKEY WAS WEIGHING scallops for Mrs. Murphy when Charlie said, "Here comes your friend."

After another night of almost no sleep, Mickey had been in a stupor all morning, feeling barely alive, but his eyes widened as he turned around suddenly, hoping to see Angelo. But then Mickey saw Chris walking toward the counter, and he let out the deep breath he'd taken.

"Yeah, gimme five pounds of the free shrimp please," Chris said.

Chris was wearing an "I'M WITH STUPID" T-shirt, with a picture of a finger pointing to the left.

"What's up?" Mickey said, turning away, closing the container of scallops.

"I got a break at work and thought I'd swing by," Chris said. "Can't you slip me some free food?"

"No."

"Come on, your boss won't catch you."

"What do you want?" Mickey snapped.

"*Somebody's* in a pissy mood," Chris said. "Wanna come by later and watch some hockey?"

"Not tonight," Mickey said.

"Why, got a date?"

Chris smiled, as if Mickey having a date was impossible.

Two new customers came into the store. Charlie took one order and Mickey took the other, two pounds of sea bass fillets for Mrs. Demback. As Mickey was cutting the fish, he said to Chris, "I'm kinda busy here."

"So you gonna come by later or what?"

"I can't," Mickey said.

"I hope you're not still pissed about the other night," Chris said, "I was just bustin' chops, having some fun. I was also ripped out of my mind. I don't even remember how I got home."

"It has nothing to do with that."

"You sure? 'Cause I hardly remember anything from that night, except you running out of that car like your dick was on fire." Chris started laughing. "Come on, you gotta admit that was a fuckin' riot. When you came out of that car, with that look on your face, and that she-man came after you. I can't believe you almost fucked that freak show."

Mrs. Dembeck looked over.

"Oops," Chris said, covering his mouth. "Sorry."

"Anything else?" Mickey asked the old woman.

"No, that'll be all," she said, still giving Chris a nasty look.

"I'll call you," Mickey said to Chris.

"Whatever," Chris said, "Hey, remember we got bowling Thursday night."

"Right," Mickey said, although he'd completely forgotten about it.

"We gotta win or we're out of the playoffs. So get some rest tonight, will ya? No cruisin' the West Side for chicks with dicks."

Laughing loudly, Chris exited. Mickey apologized to Mrs. Dembeck as he rang up her order at the register. After Charlie was through with his customer, he said to Mickey, "Your friend better watch his mouth."

"Who, Chris?"

"I'm telling you, man," Charlie said. "Guy like that says the wrong thing to the wrong dude, he winds up gettin' popped."

"Chris is Chris," Mickey said. "That's just the way he is."

Mickey continued to serve customers. At two o'clock there was still no sign of Angelo.

"I'm taking lunch," Mickey said to Charlie.

It was busy—five customers lined up to order.

Charlie said, "Come on, can't you wait?"

Mickey left the store.

MICKEY CALLED ARTIE from a phone booth on Flatbush and K.

"You stupid fuckin' piece of shit," Artie said.

"Relax," Mickey said.

"Relax?" Artie said. "I get on the phone with Nick this morning, he goes, 'So Mickey Prada's friend Angelo lost again last night,' and I go, 'Again?' I swear I almost had a fuckin' stroke. That's the thanks I get—gettin' you a fuckin' extension. Nick, you should've heard what he said about you. He wanted to send somebody after you to collect, but I told him, 'Lemme take care of it.' Maybe I did the wrong thing—maybe I should've let somebody come over to knock you around—teach you a lesson for going behind my back."

"I have the money," Mickey said.

"You better have the money, you dumb fuck," Artie said. "You better have it today too."

"You told me Wednesday."

"*Today.*"

"How about Thursday night? I'll come by the bookie joint."

"Do you have the money or don't you?"

"I have it, I have it."

"What, don't tell me your mobster friend came through?"

"Yeah, he did," Mickey lied.

"You know, I don't really give a shit," Artie said. "I just better see you Thursday."

"Artie, I'm sorry."

"Fuck you too," Artie said.

WHEN SAL PRADA started acting confused during dinner, talking about Mickey's mother as if she were still alive, Mickey couldn't take it anymore.

"She's dead!" he screamed. "She's fucking dead, and you're dead too! You're a living fucking vegetable!"

Mickey went into his room and locked the door. The room seemed smaller than it ever had before. It felt like there was no air to breathe, either, and there was a musty, stale odor. Mickey opened a window but it hardly helped.

Mickey turned on the TV and turned it right off. He was sick of TV—he was sick of his whole life. He thought about his friends from high school—Robert, Mark, and Steve— who had gone away to college this year. Robert was at Boston College, Mark was at U-Mass, and Steve was at SUNY-Albany. They lived in dorms, with good-looking girls around all the time, and they were busy with school and going to parties and making new friends. Mickey couldn't imagine what it would be like to live someplace else, in a different city. He couldn't even imagine what it would be like to have a different room.

When Rhonda came to the phone, Mickey wished he hadn't called her. By the way she said "Oh, hi," sounding like she might have forgotten who he was, he knew he'd made a big mistake. But he started talking to her, anyway. It was hard at first, trying to think of things to say, but after a while the conversation became more natural and he even started laughing, having a good time, forgetting he was talk-ing to a girl he hardly knew. He even managed to forget about his trouble with Angelo.

Mickey and Rhonda went on talking about Brooklyn— where they had grown up and what schools they had gone to—and about movies and TV shows. She was a big *Honey-mooners* fan. She knew as many lines from the show as Mickey did, and when she did a perfect Alice Cramden, saying, "I call you killer 'cause you slay me," Mickey didn't miss a beat, putting on his Ralph Cramden voice, firing back, "And I'm callin' Bellevue 'cause you're nuts!" When Mickey looked at the clock, he was surprised to see he had been on the phone with her for over an hour.

"So do you want to go out to dinner Friday night?" Mickey asked.

"I'd love to," Rhonda said.

He arranged to pick her up at her house at eight o'clock. After he hung up, he was excited for a while, then he thought, Who am I kidding? Rhonda had said that she was a freshman at Brooklyn College, studying English, which had always been Mickey's worst subject. He hated reading books, except sports books, and in school he'd always read the *Cliff Notes* instead of the books that were assigned to him. She also said that she lived on East Twenty-third Street, a much nicer neighborhood than where Mickey lived. He knew he would have nothing in common with an English major who probably came from a perfect family. He imagined sitting across from her at the restaurant on Friday with nothing to say. It would probably be the worst night of his life.

BY THURSDAY AFTERNOON, as Mickey expected, Angelo didn't show up to clear his debt. Now Mickey had no choice—he had to pay off Artie with his own money, and there wasn't a damn thing he could do about it.

At the Flatbush Federal Savings Bank on Flatbush and Hillel, Mickey filled out a withdrawal slip for eleven hundred dollars. Even though this was about a thousand dollars less than his debt and he had about another nine hundred in his account, he didn't want to give away *all* of his money. He figured he would just have to work out a payment plan with Artie for the difference.

Mickey slid his bankbook and the withdrawal slip under

the Plexiglas window, feeling like he was being robbed. As he watched the teller count out the hundred-dollar bills, he remembered the day he had opened the account, when he was nine years old. Mickey had won thirty-two dollars at the racetrack the week before, and his father took him to the bank one afternoon to set up a custodial account. After that, whenever he had extra cash he made deposits. He'd spent hours alone in his room, looking through his bankbook, imagining his money growing to one hundred thousand dollars or more someday. But now all the time and energy he had spent saving his money had come to nothing.

Mickey was amazed how half of his life savings fit into a single legal-size envelope. As he headed back to work, walking slowly and dejectedly along Flatbush Avenue, Mickey hoped Angelo was really in the mob. At least then he would know that he hadn't given away his money for no reason; he would know he'd had no choice.

Charlie had taken the afternoon off work to go visit his cousin at Coney Island Hospital. When Mickey returned to the fish store from the bank, Harry was working up front, serving a customer, some old lady.

"Hey, Big Bird, don't disappear on me, I gotta talk to you."

Ignoring Harry, Mickey went to the back and put on his apron.

"Hey, where you going?" Harry called after him.

When Mickey returned to the front, the customer was gone.

"What the hell's wrong with you?" Harry said.

"Leave me alone," Mickey said.

"You kiddin' me?" Harry said. "You talk to me like that again, I don't give a shit, you're outta here."

"How about the way you always talk to me?" Mickey said suddenly.

"What?" Harry said. "What the fuck're you talking about?"

"Not just today—all the time, every day at this goddamn job, I'm fuckin' sick of it!"

"You're so sick of it, there's the fuckin' door. You ever fuckin' curse at me again, you can leave, see if I give a shit!"

Mickey thought about it—walking out, never seeing Harry or reeking of fish again. It seemed like a great idea, until he remembered that he was about to give away his life savings to a bookie and that he couldn't afford to lose his job.

"I don't care what you're sick of," Harry went on. "I'm your boss and you're my employee, and if you say anything like that again you're fuckin' gone. Got that?"

"Yeah."

"What's that?"

"Yes," Mickey said louder.

"Good, and don't forget it. Now, what I had to say to you, we have a little issue here in the store I wanna talk to you about. You listening to me?"

Mickey stopped what he was doing and looked at Harry.

"Somebody's been taking from the register," Harry said. "A little over a hundred was missing one day last week. Yesterday another eighty was gone. I know you're not doing it and I know I didn't do it, so that only leaves one person."

"There has to be a mistake," Mickey said.

Harry was shaking his head. "Nope, there's no mistake. This didn't just happen one time, it happened twice. Charlie didn't say anything to you about this, did he?"

"I'm telling you, Charlie wouldn't steal," Mickey said.

"Well, somebody did. If it wasn't me and it wasn't you—"

"It wasn't Charlie, either. There's no way."

"I don't want to believe it myself," Harry said. "I mean I like the guy, but I guess I should've expected it."

"What do you mean?"

"You don't gotta have a degree to figure it out," Harry said. "Charlie comes from a lower-income family, right? He also seems to have a lot of anger in him, singing those rap lyrics all the time, and then with what happened the other night. Maybe he wants to get back at white people, so he stole from me. Look, I'm no shrink—I can't analyze the guy. All I know is money's missing from my cash register, and it didn't just dissolve into thin air."

"I don't care what you say," Mickey said, "I know Charlie, and I know he wouldn't do something like this."

"Okay, you're friends with him, right?" Harry said. "Why don't you talk to him and see what he has to say for himself?"

"I'm not gonna accuse him," Mickey said.

"Okay, then I guess I'll just have to fire him."

"You can't do that."

"Why can't I? It's not like you gotta be Albert fuckin' Einstein to clean fish. I'll put a sign in the window, and high school kids'll be lining up for his job. . . . Hey, don't get me wrong. I don't want to can the guy, but I'm not gonna let a thief work for me, either."

"All right, I'll ask him," Mickey said.

"Good," Harry said. "Now, get back to work, will ya? And if I hear any more shit come outta your mouth, I'm gonna put out *two* help-wanted signs."

AFTER MICKEY DROPPED off dinner for his father—pepper steak from the Chinese takeout on Nostrand—he drove to the bookie joint and met Artie. They went downstairs to the vestibule and Mickey gave Artie the envelope. Artie complained about the missing $1,020 and he warned Mickey that Nick would charge interest.

"How much juice we talking about?" Mickey asked.

"Dunno," Artie said, "maybe twenty, thirty percent a week—Nick's still pretty pissed off. But what do you care? It's not your money. You should just feel lucky. If Angelo didn't come through, you coulda got hung out to dry for the whole figure."

"Yeah," Mickey said, "that *was* lucky."

Later, when Mickey arrived at the bowling alley, he realized he had forgotten his bowling ball at home. It was too late to drive back to get it because his team was scheduled to play in five minutes.

"Ah, come on," Filippo said when he found out. "The guy leaves his ball home for the biggest game of the year. Now we're gonna lose thanks to that fuckin' faggot."

Glaring at Filippo, Mickey said, "It's no big deal. I'll find another ball to use."

"You can borrow mine," Chris said. "You got the same finger size as me. But I was fingerin' this girl last night, so it might be a little sticky inside there."

Chris laughed. Filippo laughed too, squeezing his balls, then he gave Chris a high five.

Mickey sat down, putting on his bowling shoes. Filippo's girlfriend Donna had come to watch the game. Donna lived around the corner from Mickey, but she was a couple of years younger and he hardly knew her. He used to know Donna's sister, Connie, though. Connie was Mickey's age and she was one of the most popular girls in junior high school. She used to go out with all the guidos, and Chris claimed that Connie was the first girl he'd had sex with, when they were in seventh grade. During her sophomore year of high school, Connie got sick, with some kind of cancer, and died about a year later.

Donna used to be shy and plain-looking, but after Connie died Donna started wearing slutty outfits, teasing up her hair as much as possible, always wearing what looked like a quarter of an inch of makeup.

While Filippo was getting his bowling shoes, Chris started talking to Donna. They were both laughing and then Chris put his arm around her shoulders.

When Filippo came back he said, "Hey, watch where those hands go."

"What?" Chris said. "There's enough to go around."

Chris and Donna both laughed, but Filippo didn't seem to think it was funny.

Chris and Donna continued talking—Chris was so into the conversation he didn't even seem to notice Mickey, sitting a few feet away from him. Meanwhile, Filippo sat next to Ralph and put on his shoes. Ralph looked over at Mickey a few times, with his lower lip hanging down.

The other team—four big, rowdy drunk guys wearing white T-shirts with "The Kings" written across the fronts—were sitting on the other side of the scorer's table.

Mickey was still feeling the pain of giving half of his life savings to Artie, and he took his anger out on the pins. He bowled his best three-game set ever—184, 204, and 244. In the third game, he had a perfect game going until the eighth frame, and a crowd gathered around watching and cheering.

The Studs won easily, by fifty-five pins, moving into second place in the standings.

"Way to go, Mick," Filippo said, patting him on the back. "I knew you were gonna have a big game tonight, stud."

"Do us a favor," Chris said, "forget your ball next week too, huh?"

Even Ralph shook Mickey's hand and spoke to Mickey, mumbling, "Good game."

When Mickey was returning his shoes, Chris came over to him and said, "Hey, we're gonna hit the diner to get something to eat. Wanna hang?"

"Why not?" Mickey said. He was in a good mood from bowling, and he didn't feel like going home.

Outside the bowling alley, Filippo was making out with Donna in the parking lot.

"Hey, save some for me," Chris said.

Filippo stopped kissing Donna, but he didn't move his mouth far away from her lips. His hands were squeezing her ass. He said, "Go ahead, I'll see you in a few."

Chris, who'd gotten a ride to the bowling alley with Filippo, went to the diner in Mickey's car, while Ralph waited for Filippo.

"So what do you think of Donna? Fuckin' hot, huh?" Chris said to Mickey in the car.

"She's all right," Mickey said.

"All right? You see that rack on her? Swear to God, they get bigger every time I see 'em. And wanna know the best part? She just turned sixteen last week. Man, I'd love to get a piece of that sometime."

They pulled into the parking lot of the Arch Diner, just up the block from the bowling alley. When they got out of the car, they breathed in the stench of raw sewage, drifting over from across the street.

Mickey and Chris sat in a booth near the window, and Maria came to take their drink orders. Maria was about forty, but she looked good for her age, with long thin legs and high pointy breasts. She was always nice to Mickey and Chris, smiling and winking at them, and calling them "sweetie" and "doll."

Mickey ordered a Coke and Chris asked for an egg cream. As usual, Chris started hitting on Maria. He told her how sexy she looked tonight, and he asked her if she'd marry him someday. Maria was a good sport, laughing and playing along, even though Mickey could tell she was sick of coming to work every night, just to get hit on by horny teenagers.

Ralph and Filippo showed up and joined Mickey and Chris in the booth.

"I shouldn'ta come here," Filippo said. "Donna wanted

me to go back to her place with her. Last night, I fucked her four times and she was begging me for more. My balls hurt so bad I couldn't fall asleep."

"You gotta be careful," Chris said. "Her old man's really protective and shit. Remember when he caught Kenny Thomas in her sister Connie's bed in eighth grade? He came after him with a baseball bat—almost broke his fuckin' head open."

"I'm not stupid," Filippo said. "I don't fuck Donna in her house. I take her to *my* house. My mother doesn't care, as long as I keep my sheets clean."

"Hey, Mickey," Chris said, "I got a joke for you. A rabbi and a priest are on an airplane, right? The plane's goin' down and there's only one parachute. So the rabbi says to the priest, 'You take the parachute, my father owns a candy store!'"

Chris started laughing hysterically at the punch line, his tongue hanging out of his mouth, and Filippo and Ralph joined in. Mickey didn't get the joke but he started laughing too.

"Sucker!" Chris yelled, pointing at Mickey. "It's not a real joke. I knew you'd fall for it."

"You're so fuckin' stupid, Mickey," Filippo said. Then, suddenly angry, he said, "What the fuck're they doin' here?"

Filippo was looking toward the front of the diner where four black guys were seated at a booth.

"It's a free country," Chris said.

"Free my ass," Filippo said. "Niggers should stay in East New York."

Filippo was about to get up when Chris said, "Come on, just get something to eat and forget about it."

"How can I forget about four spooks sittin' behind me?"

"Come on," Chris said.

Filippo settled down and said, "Two nights ago I was out drivin' with Kenny, drinkin' beers, when we saw this nigger walkin' up K and Forty-third—right in our fuckin' neighborhood. So I say, 'Check this out,' and I went up on the sidewalk. You shoulda seen the spook's face when he saw this car on the sidewalk, comin' up behind him." Filippo laughed. "He got away, but it was still a fuckin' riot."

"So what're you guys having, I'm starving," Chris said, looking at his menu.

"We shoulda pulled a Mill Basin on that nigger," Filippo said. "You hear about that the other night? They beat the shit outta those niggers with a fuckin' baseball bat? Serves 'em right—fuckin' spook bastards, tryin' to fuck our girlfriends."

"Shut up," Mickey said.

Filippo stared at Mickey, looking shocked. "What'd you just say?"

"You heard me," Mickey said. "I'm sick of listening to your bullshit, so why don't you just shut up?"

Filippo leaned over the table and tried to punch Mickey. Mickey moved back in time and the fist breezed past his face.

"Come on, chill out," Chris said to Filippo.

Filippo laughed. "Scared you, huh?" he said to Mickey. "What's the matter? You a nigger lover *and* a faggot now?"

"I work with one of the guys who got attacked that night, all right?" Mickey said.

"Holy shit," Chris said to Mickey. "Why didn't you tell me?"

"It was *that* guy?" Filippo said. "I never liked that fuckin' nigger—always looks at me like Kunta Kinte when I buy fish from him. I always wondered why they hired a nigger at that fish store in the first place. I mean why wouldn't the owner of the store just hire a normal white guy?"

Mickey shook his head, looking out the window.

"I was just curious," Filippo said to Mickey, "what's it like workin' with a spook all day? He teaching you all about watermelons and fried chicken?"

"All right, leave him alone," Chris said.

"Ooh, look how mad I'm gettin' him," Filippo said to Mickey, smiling. "What's the matter? You and that nigger queer together now or what?"

"Give him a break," Chris said.

"What? I'm just asking him a question," Filippo said. "The guy has a mouth—he can use it."

"Come on, just leave him alone," Chris said. "He bowled good for us tonight, didn't he?"

"Yeah," Filippo said, "but that don't mean Mickey Mouse here don't suck black dick."

"Come on," Chris said, "let's get cute Maria back here so we can order."

"He's right," Mickey said, putting down his menu.

"Right about what?" Filippo said.

"Charlie and me," Mickey said. "We try to keep it a secret, you know, but during the day we go to the back room together and fuck each other's brains out."

"See? What did I tell you?" Filippo said to Ralph.

Ralph just sat there, staring.

"He's bullshitting you," Chris said to Filippo.

"Nah, I can tell he's telling the truth," Filippo said. "I always knew he was queer—since he was a little kid. Remember when we were kids we used to play hockey in the street sometimes? Mickey would never play with us. That's because it was too rough for him. He was probably sitting home in his room, playing with his Barbie dolls."

"You're right, I was," Mickey said. "I have a whole Barbie doll collection. I have a Ken doll too. But I play with Ken a lot more than Barbie."

"I don't even wanna sit at the table with this fuckin' guy no more," Filippo said. "I might catch AIDS."

"What's AIDS?" Chris asked.

"Some new faggot disease they got," Filippo said. "If you shake hands with a faggot you die."

"Come on, let's just order some food," Chris said.

"And I knew that nigger he works with was a fudgepacker too," Filippo said. "He always walks funny, like he's got dicks up his ass."

"Fuck you," Mickey said.

"What?" Filippo said. "You don't like it when I make fun of your boyfriend? You want me to call him a spearchucker instead?"

Mickey glared at Filippo.

"What're you gonna do," Filippo said, "hit me with your nail file? Or you gonna call your monkey boyfriend to come beat me up?"

Mickey tried to go after Filippo, climbing over the table. Chris leaned over, holding Mickey back.

"Don't hit me," Filippo begged. "Please don't hit me! I don't wanna die from AIDS. Please! Please!"

"Come on, you douche bags," Chris said. "You wanna get tossed from here or what?"

Mickey stood up, put two bucks on the table, and headed toward the door.

"Hey, where you going?" Chris said. "Come on."

Mickey left the diner and headed toward his car at the end of the parking lot.

"Hey, Mickey!" Chris called out from behind him. "Mickey!"

Mickey didn't turn around. As he was getting into his car, Chris grabbed his shoulder from behind.

"Lemme go," Mickey said.

"Come on," Chris said. "Come back inside."

"Fuck you. I'm going home."

"Don't pay attention to Filippo. You know he's just full of shit."

"I don't care about Filippo."

"Then what's wrong?"

"Just leave me alone, all right?"

"Lighten up, man," Chris said. "Jesus, you're eighteen and you sound like my fuckin' grandfather. I don't know what's wrong with you."

"You wanna know what's wrong with me?" Mickey said. "I lost half my life savings today—how's that for having something wrong with me? Now can you lemme get the fuck outta here?"

"What're you talking about?"

Mickey hadn't meant to tell Chris about the money he'd given to Artie, and he was sorry he had.

"Forget it," Mickey said.

"No, tell me, what'd you do," Chris said, "blow all your money at the track?"

Figuring it didn't make a difference now, anyway, Mickey told Chris what had been going on.

Afterward Chris said, "You're such a fuckin' idiot. Why did you put in bets for him?"

"Fuck you," Mickey said.

Mickey got in his car and slammed the door. As he was warming up the engine, Chris knocked on the window. Mickey rolled his eyes, then cranked the window open.

"I can't believe you took money out of the bank," Chris said. "Why didn't you come to me first?"

"What for?"

Mickey started to close the window. Chris put his hand over it.

"You want your money back?" Chris said. "Because if you do, I can help you get it."

"What the hell're you talking about?" Mickey said.

Chris looked over his shoulder to make sure no one was around, then he said, "I can't give you your money back, but I can help you get it. Me, Ralph, and Filippo—we've been doing this thing. I've been putting away under my mattress, saving up for a new Firebird."

"What's the *thing?*"

"Just a thing to make money. If you get in on it, you might be able to make back all the money you lost today in a week, or in a day if you're lucky. I don't think they'll want you in, but they'll let you in if I put my foot down, and I will if you want me to."

"Is it something illegal?"

"You said you want your money back, right?"

Mickey stared at Chris for a few seconds, then said, "Lemme go."

Chris moved his hand from the window, then stood there, watching Mickey drive away.

WHEN MICKEY OPENED the outer door to his apartment, he was greeted by the odor of urine. Blackie, Mickey's landlord's dog, had a bladder problem and sometimes couldn't hold it in before he got outside.

Blackie started barking venomously as Mickey headed up the dark steep stairwell, leading to the door to his apartment. Mickey opened the door and reached for the light switch when someone grabbed him and pushed him against the wall, and Mickey felt the sharp edge of a knife against his chin.

The person holding Mickey was breathing heavily, panting.

"Dad?" Mickey said weakly.

"What the hell're you doing in this apartment? Huh? You trying to rob us?"

"It's me, Dad. It's Mickey."

"Who? What the hell're you talking about you son of a bitch?"

Mickey felt the tip of the blade going into his chin, and he realized that his father could easily slit his throat.

Mickey grabbed his father's wrist, above the hand that was holding the knife, and squeezed as hard as he could.

"You fuckin' bastard," Sal Prada said.

When the tip of the knife was no longer piercing his skin, Mickey kneed his father in the balls. Sal grunted, then Mickey heard the knife fall onto the floor. Mickey went to his knees and felt around. The apartment wasn't completely dark—there was some light coming from the lampposts outside—but Mickey's eyes hadn't adjusted yet and he could barely see. Finally, Mickey felt the blade part of the knife, but before he could grip the handle, his father grabbed it. Mickey went for his father's wrist again; he could only squeeze with his right hand, the one without the stitches. They struggled on the floor. Mickey didn't know where the knife was, and he was afraid it would go into his chest.

"Let go!" Mickey yelled. "Just let go!"

Mickey caught a glimpse of his father's face—Sal Prada looked like a maniac, with his teeth clenched and his eyes wide open. Sal lunged forward and Mickey felt a slash on his left arm, above his elbow.

"Fuckin' idiot!" Mickey yelled. "What the hell's wrong with you?!"

Sal tried to stab Mickey again, but this time Mickey saw the blade coming. He grabbed the handle, over his father's hand, and gradually managed to pry his father's fingers loose. Finally, Mickey freed the knife. He stood up and his father grabbed one of Mickey's legs. Mickey kicked his father in the head and his father let go. Mickey went to the end of the hallway and turned on the hallway light.

Sal Prada stood there, looking confused. Mickey checked

his arm—it was bleeding, but the cut wasn't as deep as he'd feared.

"You could've killed me, you fuckin' moron," Mickey said. "Are you out of your fuckin' mind?"

"What're you doing here?" Sal said. "There was a guy breaking into the house. I saw him breaking in."

Mickey went into the bathroom and rinsed his arm in the sink. The bleeding stopped quickly, but he knew it could have been a lot worse.

Dressing the wound, he decided he couldn't live this way anymore. He was going to put his father away in a home, like he should've a long time ago. That would solve problem number one. But he would still need money, to pay off the rest of the debt to Artie and to pay for his own expenses when he started college next year.

Mickey watched the end of the ten o'clock news, then he watched *The Odd Couple,* the one where Oscar goes to the fat farm. Mickey had seen the episode dozens of times before, and he just lay in bed in the dark, staring at the screen, hardly paying attention.

During *The Honeymooners*—the one where Ralph takes his boss out to dinner and tries to pick up the check he can't afford—Mickey called Chris.

"I just walked in the door," Chris said.

"About that thing we were talking about before in the parking lot," Mickey said.

"What about it?"

"I want in," Mickey said.

7

CHRIS WAS WAITING by his front door.

"My mom's home, let's go up to my room," Chris said.

Mickey followed Chris past the living room, where Mrs. Turner was sprawled out on the couch in her nightgown with the TV going and a bottle of gin on the floor nearby. Her mouth was halfway open and she was snoring loudly. She used to be good-looking with long blonde hair and always wore tight, sexy outfits. Now she'd put on about fifty pounds, her face was wrinkled and drawn, and she had short graying hair.

In Chris's room, Chris locked the door and cleared some dirty laundry off of a chair and told Mickey to sit down. Posters of Rush, Led Zeppelin, and Gladys Portuguese hung on the far wall, and the latest centerfolds from *Penthouse* and *Hustler* were thumbtacked to the wall above Chris's bed.

Chris sat down on the bed across from Mickey and said, "So what made you change your mind?"

"I don't know if I changed my mind," Mickey said. "I just want to hear what the thing is first."

"I can't tell you anything unless you really want in," Chris said. "I talked to Ralph and Filippo at the diner—they okay'd it, but I need your word."

"Come on, just tell me," Mickey said.

Chris waited then said, "We're gonna rob a house in Manhattan Beach."

"You're kidding me," Mickey said.

"What?" Chris said.

"That's *it?*" Mickey said.

"Just hear me out, will ya?"

"I think I've heard enough."

"Just listen. We're not just gonna go to some house, ring the bell, and if no one answers break in. We're not stupid. We've got it all figured out. We know nobody's gonna be there, we know what's in the house, and we know exactly how to get in and out."

"Yeah?" Mickey said. "And how do you know all this?"

"Because Filippo's cousin lives there."

"His cousin?"

"The guy and his wife are gonna be away at the Poconos for the weekend," Chris said. "They got another house up there—you know, a country house—and they go away all the time. They leave Friday, come back Sunday. So on Saturday nobody's gonna be home."

"So let me get this straight," Mickey said. "Filippo wants to rob his own cousin?"

"He's rich as hell," Chris said.

"It's still his cousin."

"He's a scumbag too," Chris said. "Filippo said he cheats on his wife all the time, sleeps with whores, you name it. And the shit we're gonna take—it's all insured. The big prize, the wife's diamond engagement ring, is two fuckin' carats, worth twenty g's easy on the street. Filippo heard his mother talking to the wife—she never wears the ring and she doesn't keep it locked up, neither. She's got other jewelry in the house too. All we gotta do is find where she keeps it, and we figure with one extra guy we got a better shot at it."

"You're out of your mind," Mickey said.

"Why?" Chris said. "We got it all figured out. Last time, I cleared a thousand bucks, but we think we got a shot at more this time."

"Who did you rob last time?"

"Filippo's grandmother."

Mickey shook his head. He couldn't believe he was even listening to this.

"We coulda done better with that one," Chris went on. "We heard a noise and left early, but we didn't have to. That's why we all think another guy might help. With another guy maybe we coulda got his grandmother's wedding band and fancy silverware and made another couple grand easy."

"I'm not gonna rob a house," Mickey said, "and I'm definitely not gonna rob Filippo's cousin."

"Hey, you were the one who called me," Chris said. "I was just trying to help you out, because I felt bad for you, but if you don't want to get all your money back plus some, that's fine. It was hard to talk Ralph and Filippo into it, anyway. They wanted to use this guy Jimmy instead, but I told them you're in or I'm out, and that finally got them. If we find the ring, we could get at least five grand each. But if you don't want a chance of getting five grand for fifteen minutes' work with absolutely no risk, that's up to you."

Mickey wanted to leave, but he kept thinking about the money—five grand, enough to pay off Artie, make a deposit in his bank account, start school in the spring, and get his whole life back on track.

"So what are you gonna do," Mickey said, "just go break the door down?"

"Nah, we're gonna blow it up with a stick of dynamite." Chris rolled his eyes. "Ralph used to work for a locksmith on Avenue U. He knows how to pick any kind of lock, and he can dismantle alarms too. Whatever we get Ralph'll bring to a fence in Queens. Let's say we come away with thirty grand worth of shit. We sell it to the fence for twenty and boom—we get five grand apiece."

"What if the police catch on?" Mickey asked.

"How could they?" Chris said.

"Gee, I don't know," Mickey said, "what if they figure out only Filippo's relatives are getting robbed?"

"It's two houses in two totally different neighborhoods in Brooklyn," Chris said. "Filippo's grandmother was Canarsie, his cousin's Manhattan Beach. The only connection is Filippo, but how would the cops figure that out? Besides, that's why we waited a month. So the two robberies would be spread apart. I'm telling you, we got all the bases covered."

Mickey imagined what it could be like—winding up with more money than he'd had before Angelo made his first bet, moving out of his father's house into his own apartment, maybe in Manhattan.

After thinking it over for about a minute, Mickey said, "So you're sure Filippo's cousin's gonna be in the Poconos, right?"

8

CHARLIE WAS AT the counter, cutting tuna steaks with one hand, his other arm with the cast by his side. Rap music was playing at a low volume from the boom box on the floor next to him.

"We've got two hands between us," Mickey said, holding up his hand with the bandaged finger.

"Don't bother me," Charlie said. "I got one hand, I do half as much work, that's all."

Working very slowly, Charlie continued to cut the tuna with one hand.

"How's your cousin doing?" Mickey asked.

"He got out of the hospital yesterday," Charlie said. "He had a concussion and a skull fracture, broke some bones. He has trouble remembering shit right now, but the docs say he'll be all right."

"That's cool," Mickey said. "I hope they catch the bastards who did it. "

"I ain't keepin' my fingers crossed," Charlie said. "Till we get a black mayor in this city, black people won't get shit from the police."

"Hey, I need to talk to you about something else," Mickey said. "It's something Harry said to me yesterday."

"If that asshole wants me to start coming in earlier, tell him forget it. I told him—I gotta take my little brother to school in the morning."

"It's not about that," Mickey said. "It's just there's kinda been a problem in the store lately. At least that's what Harry says."

Charlie stopped working, holding the knife by his side. He said, "What kinda problem?"

"Harry said there was some money missing from the register."

"Don't surprise me," Charlie said, turning back away from Mickey, slicing into the fish again. "The guy's the dumbest motherfucker in the world—he probably don't even know his times tables yet. You think he can count money from a cash register?"

"I don't really care," Mickey said, "but Harry said it's happened twice."

"So maybe he made a mistake twice," Charlie said. "Wouldn't be the first time that man had his head up his ass."

"Yeah," Mickey said, "you're probably right."

Later, Harry returned to the store to close up and Charlie left before Mickey.

"So," Harry said to Mickey as soon as Charlie was gone. "Did you find anything out?"

"He said he didn't do it," Mickey said.

"Figures," Harry said. "The guy's a born thief *and* a born liar. Well, you did your best. I guess we'll just have to catch him in the act."

MICKEY HADN'T THOUGHT much about Rhonda since getting off the phone with her the other day, but when he arrived home from work he was surprisingly nervous about their date tonight. He showered, washing his hair twice and scrubbing himself with soap and rinsing off several times, trying to get the fish odor off of his body. He thought he got most of it out but he put on extra Old Spice, under his arms and all over his back, chest, and stomach just in case.

He cut himself shaving in a few places and had to cover the cuts with tiny pieces of toilet paper to stop the bleeding. In his room, he was about to get dressed when he realized he didn't have any nice clothes to wear. He wished he'd thought about this sooner—he could have gone shopping, bought a new pair of pants at least. He put on a red pin-striped shirt, which was too tight on him, and beige corduroys, which were definitely out of style. He didn't have anything better to wear and it was too late to try to find a new outfit, so he decided he'd just have to make the best of it. Cursing, he brushed his hair, catching a whiff of his breath. He'd had a slice of pizza with pepperoni and sausage on it for lunch, and he needed to brush his teeth. He was on his way to the bathroom when he saw the thick smoke in the hallway. Covering his mouth, he went into the kitchen and found the source of the smoke—two smoldering whole fish on a frying pan. He shut the flame and put the frying pan in the sink, creating a huge rush of fishy smoke that went right up to his face.

"Dad!" Mickey yelled. "Dad!"

Sal Prada came running into the kitchen.

"What the hell's going on?" he said. "You trying to burn down the fuckin' umbrella?"

"The what?"

"You started a fuckin' fire."

"*You* did this," Mickey said. "You left the fuckin' frying pan on the stove."

"I never put any frying pan on the stove, you lying son of a bitch."

"I've had it with this shit," Mickey said. "Next week you're outta here—I'm putting you in a fuckin' home where you belong!"

"Hey, where the hell do you think you're going? What about my dinner?"

Mickey went to his room to get his wallet, then he pushed past his father, who was still screaming at him, and left the apartment. The inside of his car needed a cleaning badly, but it was already after eight o'clock, the time he was supposed to meet Rhonda. He pushed the biggest pieces of garbage—a pizza box, a potato chip bag, a Whopper wrapper—under the front seat.

As Mickey drove down Avenue I, past Bedford Avenue, the houses got bigger and nicer. There were more trees on the blocks—some of them still had orange and red leaves—and there were large front lawns with tall bushes and flower beds. In Mickey's neighborhood, most people didn't have front lawns—there was just fenced-in concrete. On Rhonda's block, there were big expensive-looking houses, and Mickey knew he didn't have to worry about feeling embarrassed around her tonight because of the way he was dressed or smelled; he had no chance with her, anyway.

He spotted Rhonda's house, one of the nicest ones on the block. It was three stories with a big front lawn and a new-looking tan Mercedes in the wide driveway.

Mickey parked in a spot across the street from the house, then he headed up the stoop and rang the bell. As he was waiting, he looked at his reflection in the little glass window on the door and saw that he had forgotten to remove the pieces of toilet paper from his face. Frantically, he tore off the toilet paper and then the door opened and a short balding man with a dark beard was standing there.

"Hi, I'm Mickey. I'm here to pick up Rhonda."

"Come in, I'm Rhonda's father," the man said without smiling. Mickey recognized the man's voice from on the phone.

The house was as nice on the inside as it was on the outside. There were fancy rugs, maybe Oriental ones, on the floor, and there were mirrors and paintings on the walls. They went into the living room, where there were two couches and a chair. Both couches were covered in plastic slipcovers. Rhonda's father sat in the chair and said, "Take a seat," motioning toward one of the couches.

As Mickey sat at the edge of the couch, the plastic crackling under him, he noticed a menorah on the mantelpiece, to the right of where Rhonda's father was sitting. Mickey hadn't even wondered if Rhonda was Jewish, but now it made sense. She didn't look Irish or Italian or anything else, and a lot of rich Jewish people lived in this neighborhood, past Bedford Avenue.

Mickey was still staring at the menorah, when Rhonda's father said, "So I understand you work at a fish store."

"Yeah, that's right," Mickey said, smelling the fish odor still on his body. "Vincent's on Flatbush Avenue. Ever been by there?"

"No, but I think I've seen it before. So is this what you plan to do with your life? Be a fishmonger?"

"No," Mickey said.

"Do you go to school?"

"Not right now," Mickey said. "But I want to start college in the spring."

"You *want* to go to college in the spring. Well, that's very ambitious."

Mickey tried to smile.

"So you finished high school I take it?" her father asked.

"Yes," Mickey said.

"So why the wait? Why not start college right away?"

"I don't know. I mean I just thought I'd take time off."

"To work in a fish store?"

"No. I mean yes. I mean I've worked in the fish store for a long time, so it's not like I took time off to work there."

"Hi, Mickey."

Rhonda was standing by the doorway. She was wearing tight jeans, a light blue fuzzy sweater, and purple plastic triangle-shaped earrings.

After staring at her for a few seconds, thinking that she

was even better-looking than he'd remembered, Mickey said, "You look great."

"Thanks . . . so do you," she said. "So you met my dad, huh?"

"Yeah, I did," Mickey said.

"Mickey and I were just discussing his college plans," Rhonda's father said.

Rhonda took a few steps toward Mickey then stopped, squinting as she looked up at Mickey's left cheek.

"I think you're bleeding," she said.

Mickey touched his cheek then looked at his index finger and saw the blood covering the tip of it.

"Sorry," he said, feeling like an idiot. "You have a bathroom?"

"Sure," Rhonda said. "It's down the hall to the right."

In the bathroom, Mickey whispered curses as he cleaned the blood off his cheek. He wanted to crawl up into a ball and die, but he finally returned to the foyer. Rhonda was waiting near the front door with her father and a very thin woman with short red hair and pale skin.

"Mickey, I'd like you to meet my stepmother, Alice."

"It's a pleasure to meet you," Alice said.

Alice smiled as she shook Mickey's hand and Rhonda's father stood off to the side.

Rhonda said good-bye to her father and stepmother, and Mickey told them how it was great to meet them and then he and Rhonda left the house.

"So I guess my father was giving you the third degree before, huh?" Rhonda said.

"No, not really," Mickey said. Then he said, "Kind of."

"I swear to God, he's so embarrassing sometimes," Rhonda said. "He acts like it's the nineteen fifties. He insists on answering the door, interrogating anybody I bring to the house."

"It's all right," Mickey said. "I'm sure he's a nice guy when you get to know him. Your stepmother seemed nice too."

"Don't let her fool you," Rhonda said. "She can be a real bitch sometimes."

Mickey opened Rhonda's door first and held it open for her. When Mickey got in, he immediately noticed his strong fish odor again, but he decided not to say anything about it, just like he wouldn't say anything about his bleeding face.

It took three turns on the ignition, but the engine finally caught and they drove away. Mickey looked over to see if Rhonda was disgusted by his car and everything else about him; surprisingly, she seemed happy.

"I should probably explain about my father," Rhonda said as they headed toward Avenue J. "See, he has this thing about me dating non-Jewish guys. You're not Jewish, right?"

"Nah," Mickey said.

"I didn't think so. I don't care one way or another, but my father is such a jerk about it. See, I grew up kind of religious. Well, not religious-religious. We were Conservative."

"Oh," Mickey said. He imagined Rhonda standing outside a temple with those guys in black top hats and the long curly sideburn hair.

"But I'm Reform now," Rhonda said. "I mean I celebrate all the Jewish holidays and everything, but that's it. My father's still kind of religious, though. So what are you?"

"Italian," Mickey said.

"That's nice," Rhonda said. "I don't really care a lot about religion. I think all people are basically the same."

Rhonda went on, talking about herself. Her mother and father had gotten divorced three years ago, and now her mother lived in Los Angeles. She was going to Brooklyn College, only because her father had pressured her to go to a school close to home, and next year she hoped to transfer to NYU or Columbia. When they arrived at Cookie's, a restaurant on Avenue M known for its big salad bar with unlimited shrimp, Mickey was amazed at how quickly time had gone by. It seemed like they had only left Rhonda's block about a minute or two ago, and there hadn't been any lulls in the conversation.

They parked around the corner from the restaurant, and Mickey went around and opened Rhonda's door for her. There was a wait to be seated, so they stood at the front of the restaurant, talking almost nonstop. Rhonda asked Mickey why he hadn't gone to college right after high school. Mickey explained about his father's Alzheimer's disease and stroke and how he'd been taking care of his father since the summer.

"I think that's so wonderful," Rhonda said.

"What is?" Mickey said.

"The way you love your father. You two must be really close."

Remembering how his father had tried to kill him the other night, Mickey said, "Yeah, I guess you can say that."

The hostess sat them at a table in the back. Rhonda asked Mickey about his mother and Mickey explained how she had been killed in a car accident on the Brooklyn-Queens Expressway.

"I'm so sorry," Rhonda said. She leaned across the table and put her hand on top of Mickey's.

"You work very hard, don't you?" she said.

Although Mickey had scrubbed his hands, they still looked dirty and had a lot of cuts and scratches.

"Sorry," he said. "My hands just get like that from cleaning fish."

"I like them," Rhonda said. "They have a lot of character."

Rhonda let go of Mickey's hand but Mickey wished she hadn't.

As they ate their salads and chicken with mashed potatoes, they continued talking and laughing. Rhonda told Mickey how she wanted to be a high school English teacher someday and travel to Europe. Mickey said he wanted to be an accountant, then he told her the story of how he got the name Mickey.

"The Yankees were playing the Orioles the day I was born. Mickey Mantle hit a homer in the ninth to win the game, so my father said to my mother, 'Let's name the kid Mickey.' For years after that my father said to me, 'You're lucky Boog Powell didn't hit one out that day.'"

Rhonda laughed and Mickey was surprised how well the date was going. Even though Rhonda knew that he didn't have any money and came from a strange family, she wasn't turned off.

For dessert, Mickey took Rhonda to Jan's on Nostrand Avenue. There were a lot of teenagers in the place, and Mickey liked how a few guys checked Rhonda out as he sat down with her at a table. They ordered "the kitchen sink," a huge bowl with every kind of ice cream and syrup inside it.

Rhonda said, "I don't want to butt into your life or anything, but can I make a suggestion?"

"Sure," Mickey said.

"There's an accounting program at Brooklyn College," Rhonda said, "and there's probably courses you could take. Why don't you take a class or two at night next semester? It probably wouldn't take too much time—I mean you could still work at the fish store during the day. Meanwhile, you could be earning credits toward a degree."

"That's a good idea," Mickey said. "But I'm gonna start school in January full time."

"You are? I thought you told me on the phone you weren't going to go until next year."

"My plans changed since then," Mickey said. "I figured, why put it off if I don't have to?"

As Rhonda went on, talking about something else, Mickey stared at her mouth. Her lips looked so good, eating the ice cream, Mickey wanted to kiss her right now—just lean across the table and get it over with.

"Are you okay?" Rhonda asked.

"Yeah, fine," Mickey said.

"Your eyes looked like they were crossing for a second," Rhonda said.

"Nah, I was just thinking about something," Mickey said. "Sorry."

"You had a long day at work—you must be tired."

"Nah, I'm fine, really," Mickey said.

Rhonda looked at her watch and yawned.

"I guess it's getting kind of late," she said.

Mickey didn't want the date to end. He wanted to take Rhonda for a long walk, maybe near Sheepshead Bay. It was nice there at night, by the docks. It would be a good place to kiss her.

"You should really take me home now," Rhonda said. "My father's gonna kill me if I get home late tonight."

"It's not late yet, is it?" Mickey said.

"Yeah, it is, it's ten-thirty already."

Mickey was surprised—it was nine o'clock the last time he'd checked his watch, which seemed like just a few minutes ago.

Mickey paid the bill at the register, then he and Rhonda went outside. On the way to the car in the parking lot, Mickey held Rhonda's hand. It felt warm and soft.

As they drove down Nostrand Avenue, Mickey couldn't get a full breath. He was trying to decide when to kiss her—in the car, or in front of her house.

"Hey, I have an idea," Rhonda said. "Do you want to teach me how to drive sometime?"

"Sure," Mickey said.

"I still have a learner's permit," Rhonda said, "but I never got around to taking a road test. And, oh my God, my father's the world's worst teacher. Seriously, he's really smart, but he can't stop looking over his shoulder while I'm driving and it makes me so nervous. But I have a feeling I'd be a lot more comfortable around you."

"I'd love to teach you," Mickey said. "Anytime."

They turned down Avenue I, then onto Rhonda's block. Mickey had been hoping to pull into a spot and make a move on her, but there were no spaces, so he had to double-park. With the motor running he looked into her eyes for a few seconds, then she said, "Well, good night."

She opened the door and started to get out. Mickey was kicking himself for blowing his chance.

Then Rhonda looked back at him and said, "You want to walk me to my door?"

"Sure," Mickey said, thanking God.

He shut the engine and went around and held Rhonda's door open for her. They walked up the concrete path toward the stoop to the house. Rhonda stopped and turned toward Mickey. Mickey was about to lean toward her when she said, "Do you like shows?"

"Shows?" Mickey said.

"Yeah, shows," Rhonda said. "You know, Broadway shows."

"I don't know," Mickey said. "I mean I've never been to one before."

"You've never been to a Broadway show?"

"Nah," Mickey said. "I mean I saw one on TV once. *Jesus Christ Superstar*."

"Oh my God, I'm definitely taking you Sunday. I have two tickets to *Cats*. I was supposed to go with my stepmother but she can't make it. You can go Sunday, can't you?"

"Sure," Mickey said.

"Great. I guess we can take the subway together or—"

"No, I can drive," Mickey said.

"Really? Okay, the show starts at three, so maybe you could come pick me up at about eleven. We can go to lunch first."

"Okay, I'll be there—I mean here."

Mickey laughed, his mouth suddenly dry. Rhonda's eyes were aimed down slightly, toward Mickey's lips. Mickey knew this was his chance, but he didn't move. He just stood still, doing nothing, and he was hating himself. Then he was doing it. His tongue was in her mouth, swirling against her tongue, and he felt like everything else disappeared—it was just their tongues and mouths and nothing else.

Mickey didn't want the kiss to end, but finally Rhonda pulled back and said, "Good night, Mickey."

"Good night," Mickey said.

Mickey watched Rhonda go into the house, and he stayed there long after the door had closed.

9

ALL DAY SATURDAY Mickey couldn't get Rhonda out of his head. He kept replaying conversations from last night, remembering how easy it was to talk to her, and how proud he was to be with her. He also remembered how good it felt to hold her hand and especially to kiss her. It wasn't like kissing other girls for the first time; he wasn't nervous at all and he'd felt like he'd kissed her hundreds of times before. At work, every time the bell above the door rang, Mickey looked up from whatever he was doing, hoping to see her, feeling the disappointment a moment later. He didn't know how he would make it until tomorrow to see her again. He wanted to be with her right now—just throw down his apron, run to her house, and hold her. He had definitely fallen in love.

Mickey was surprised because he had thought it would be years before he fell in love, and he didn't expect it would be with someone like Rhonda. He'd always imagined his future wife as a simple, plain-looking girl. She wouldn't be ugly, but she wouldn't be beautiful, either. She would be a nice girl, though, someone he got along with, anyway, and they would get together because they were tired of being alone and just wanted to settle down and start a family. But now he had Rhonda, the type of girl he'd never thought would like him. She was beautiful, smart, funny, and the best part was that she seemed to like him as much as he liked her. He imagined how great it would be in the spring, when he had started college and they could go to the library, or just hang out in a park somewhere and study together. Then, next year, she might be going to NYU or Columbia, and they could ride to the city together on the subway, meeting for lunch and dinner all the time.

At one point in the afternoon, Mickey was staring out the front window, daydreaming, when Harry came up behind him and said, "Hey, space cadet, what's the matter, forget to plug in your brain today? I just told you to go mop the bathroom floor—the pipe in the ceiling's leaking again."

Mickey smiled; even Harry couldn't ruin his great mood.

Later, at home, Mickey thought about calling Rhonda, just to say hi and tell her that he'd had a great time last night. But he wasn't sure it was right to call so early, just a day after the first date, so he watched TV instead.

At nine o'clock, Mickey couldn't take it anymore.

"Rhonda, it's Mickey."

"Mickey," Rhonda said, "I'm so glad you called. It's about tomorrow."

"You can't make it," Mickey said, feeling the letdown.

"No, of course I can make it. It's just my father being a jerk. It's nothing personal against you—it's just the way he is. I'm sure after a little time goes by he won't mind, but tomorrow can you pick me up at the corner of Bedford and J just so he doesn't get mad."

"No problem," Mickey said.

Mickey had only planned to stay on the phone with Rhonda for a couple of minutes, but they started talking and the conversation didn't stop. Rhonda told Mickey about her brother who had died of a brain tumor when he was twelve, then Mickey told her more about his mother's car accident. He told her how he'd been afraid to get in cars for weeks after she was killed and how hard it was to grow up alone with his father. Mickey had never talked to anyone about personal things before, and it felt strange and good to open up.

Later in the conversation, Mickey and Rhonda realized that they knew someone in common. In fourth grade, Mickey had a friend named Ronny Feldman. Rhonda had gone to day camp with Ronny the year before, and Mickey and Rhonda had both gone to Ronny's ninth birthday party. While Mickey was on the phone, Rhonda found a picture she had from the party where she and Mickey were standing right next to each other. Rhonda said, "See, it must've been fate that we met," and she promised to bring the picture with her tomorrow.

Mickey wanted to stay on the phone, but he glanced at the clock and saw that it was past eleven. He couldn't believe they had been talking for over two hours.

Mickey said good-bye and then wound up staying on the phone for another fifteen minutes before finally hanging up. He felt light-headed yet full of energy, the same way he'd felt driving home after the date last night.

Still pleasantly dazed, Mickey started getting dressed to meet Chris and the guys.

AT A COUPLE minutes before midnight, Mickey, in black pants, black shoes, and a navy parka, left his house and walked across the street to Chris's, where a new-looking red Buick Skyhawk with Jersey plates was waiting double-parked.

When Mickey was a few feet away from the car, Chris opened the back door and said, "Hold it."

Mickey stopped and then Chris tossed him a pair of yellow dishwashing gloves.

"Put these on first," Chris said. "We don't wanna get your prints in the car."

As Mickey was putting on the gloves, Chris said, "What's with the coat? Didn't I tell you to wear all black?"

"I don't have a black coat."

"Whatever," Chris said.

Chris slid over. Mickey hesitated, then he got in the car and closed the door. Ralph was in the driver's seat and Filippo was riding shotgun. Ralph started the car and drove away.

"I got everything you need," Chris said to Mickey. "Here's your ski mask—put it on inside the house. Here's your flashlight—same thing, inside the house. And here's your laundry bag to fill up with shit."

Chris sat back, looking straight ahead very seriously. Ralph turned up the stereo—some oldies station playing "Daydream Believer." A few minutes went by and no one said a word. Mickey was surprised because Chris hated sixties music and he'd usually complain until Ralph changed the station, and Filippo usually wouldn't shut up.

When Frankie Valli came on singing "Big Girls Don't Cry" everyone was still quiet and serious, acting like they were on their way to a funeral.

Mickey wanted to tell Ralph to stop the car. At the next red light, he could get out, walk home, and forget about the whole thing. The car stopped and Mickey put his hand on the door handle, but he couldn't turn it. He was thinking about the money they might get from the ring and his take—five thousand dollars. He'd have to be crazy to get out now.

Driving down Ocean Avenue, the sixties music went on and Mickey sat in the back of the car, as quiet and serious as everyone else.

THE HOUSES IN Manhattan Beach were even bigger and more expensive than the ones in Rhonda's neighborhood. Filippo's cousin lived in a huge three-story house with a big front lawn and stained-glass windows. Mickey figured the place must have cost a half a million bucks easy. Mickey couldn't imagine what it would be like to grow up in one of these houses, with all that space, never having to worry about anything.

Ralph shut off the ignition, the headlights, and the radio. Suddenly, it was almost totally quiet, as if they were parked on a country road instead of on a street in Brooklyn.

"Okay," Filippo said. "Everybody ready?"

"Remember," Chris said to Mickey, "you and Ralph got

the first floor, me and Filippo are gonna take the second and third floors. Ralph's gonna get out of the car first and take care of the lock and the alarm. He's gonna go in through the door in the back, then he's gonna come out and open the front door. When the front door opens we all move. But not fast—we *walk* across the street to the house. When we get into the house, we put on our ski masks and get to work. Ralph's on lookout. If he yells, 'Let's go,' that's it, we leave. Remember, take whatever you think we can get money for, but it can't be too big. Whatever we take's gotta fit into the laundry bags. No TV sets, no stereos. Got it?"

Mickey didn't say anything.

"Okay," Chris said. "Here we go."

Ralph got out of the car, carrying his rolled-up laundry bag, ski mask, and flashlight. He walked casually across the street, looking like a guy on his way home from work, or just passing by on his way to visit a friend. He went up the driveway and disappeared behind the house.

In the car, nobody said a word. Mickey wasn't wearing a watch, but he figured about five minutes must have gone by since Ralph had gone around the house. Chris was taking deep breaths, but up front Filippo was still.

After another few minutes passed, Filippo said, "What the fuck's taking him so long?"

"Relax, will ya?" Chris said. "He knows what he's doing."

Chris sounded nervous, Mickey thought, not nearly as confident as he had the other night when he was talking about the robbery.

Another few minutes went by and then, finally, Ralph poked his head out of the front door of the house.

"All right, let's do it," Chris said.

Filippo left the car first and headed across the street, and Chris and Mickey followed. The air was clean and fresh—the Atlantic was just a few blocks away—and Mickey took deep breaths, trying to stay calm.

At the top of the stoop, they put on their ski masks, and then they entered the house. It was almost pitch-dark inside and they turned on their flashlights right away. Chris followed Filippo straight ahead, toward the staircase, and they went up. Mickey stayed on the first floor with Ralph. Ralph was busy, looking for stuff in the living room, so Mickey went into the dining room. He opened the drawers to all the cabinets of a big armoire, searching for anything that looked valuable. In the first two drawers, he couldn't find anything, but in the third he found a bunch of old stamps in a box and he dropped the box inside the laundry bag. In a cabinet in the dining room he found a Polaroid camera. Continuing on, he shined his flashlight on a framed picture of a couple on a beach. They looked like they were in their forties—the guy heavyset with dark hair, a little gray in it, in a bathing suit; the woman, also heavy but with blonde hair, wearing a bikini.

Mickey finished in the dining room and went into the kitchen. He searched a few drawers and didn't find anything worth taking. In a cabinet above the refrigerator he found a box of fancy-looking silverware and he added it to the laundry bag, but he couldn't find anything else. He went into the next room, a den, and started looking around. There was a Betamax hooked up to a TV. Mickey knelt down, unplugged the wires, and put it inside the laundry bag. He saw some videocassettes nearby on the floor, but he figured they weren't worth taking, then he shined his flashlight on top of the TV and spotted a watch—a Rolex. His heart started pounding, as if he'd just hit the triple at the track. The watch had to be worth a thousand bucks, maybe more. He dropped it in the bag and started on the other side of the room. He opened a drawer to a desk and saw coins—silver dollars mostly, about twenty of them. He scooped them out and dropped them in the bag, when he heard what sounded like a gunshot. He dropped the laundry bag on the floor, then there was another shot. It sounded like both shots had come from upstairs. He picked up the laundry bag and rushed to the foyer, near the staircase. His mind was churning too fast to think clearly. He'd never heard live gunshots and he hoped that he'd made a mistake—it was just a car backfiring or kids playing with firecrackers.

He shined his flashlight up the stairs and saw nothing. Then he shined his light around downstairs in every direction, wondering where Ralph was.

"Ralph," Mickey whispered, but there was no answer.

Mickey wondered if Ralph had taken off. The front door was right behind Mickey. He thought about running himself, but decided not to. Not without Chris, anyway.

Mickey whispered loudly, "Chris," but there was no answer. He said it again, louder, and there was still nothing. He tried calling for Ralph and Filippo, but that didn't get a response, either. Seconds went by, although they seemed like minutes. Mickey thought about going upstairs. No, it was better to stay near the front door, just in case.

Then Mickey heard a noise behind him, coming from outside the house. It sounded like someone was out there.

Mickey put the laundry bag down on the floor next to him and turned off his flashlight. He stood still, listening for another sound from outside, when he heard a different noise behind him. He turned around quickly and shined the flashlight toward Ralph and Filippo coming down the stairs. They were holding Chris upright between them.

"Get that shit outta my face," Filippo whispered harshly. He was still wearing his ski mask, and Mickey could see his squinting eyes through the holes.

Mickey shined the light away, toward the floor.

"What the fuck happened?" Mickey whispered.

No one answered. Mickey waited until they were at the bottom of the stairs, then he shined his flashlight straight ahead again, directly on Chris's blood-soaked shirt. Shifting the light higher, he saw Chris's head, still covered with the ski mask and tilted limply to one side. Blood was dripping out of Chris's mouth and his eyes were half shut. Suddenly, Mickey felt dizzy and numb and everything went white.

Filippo and Ralph, still holding up Chris between them, walked past Mickey, toward the front door.

"Wait." Mickey was breathing heavily now, barely able to talk. If he hadn't grabbed onto the banister he might have passed out. "I think . . . I think someone's out there."

Filippo and Ralph stopped and looked at each other. Then Ralph put his index finger up to his lip. Filippo held up Chris on his own while Ralph went toward the front door, aiming his gun.

Filippo shut off his flashlight then whispered to Mickey, "Shut your fuckin' light, you dick."

Mickey shut the flashlight and stood next to Filippo in the dark.

After about a minute Ralph returned and said, "I don't see nobody there."

"Fuck it," Filippo said, "Let's just get outta here—fast. And keep the masks on."

Filippo and Ralph, carrying Chris's body between them, walked ahead of Mickey. Ralph opened the door slowly with his gun drawn, checked both directions, then he and Filippo exited the house. Over their free shoulders, Ralph was carrying his laundry bag and Filippo had two laundry bags—his own and Chris's. Mickey followed, carrying his own laundry bag slung over one shoulder.

It seemed to take forever to cross the street, but they finally made it to the car. Ralph opened the back door and put Chris's body inside, sitting him upright as if he were still alive. Mickey felt like he might throw up. Ralph opened the trunk and everyone dumped their laundry bags inside, when an old man's voice said, "Hey, what's going on over there?"

The voice sounded close by, maybe the guy was across the street, but Mickey didn't check to see.

Ralph and Filippo scrambled to get in the front of the car, and Mickey got in the back next to Chris's body. One of Mickey's legs was still outside the door as the car pulled away, but he managed to get his entire body inside and close the door as the car peeled up the block.

At the corner, Ralph made a sharp left onto Shore Boulevard, and Chris's body shifted onto Mickey. Mickey pushed it away frantically.

"Chill out," Filippo said to Ralph, "the last thing we need is to get pulled over for speeding."

Ralph slowed down, but he still seemed to be going about sixty.

"What the fuck happened up there?" Mickey asked, looking away from Chris, out the window.

No one answered.

"I said what the fuck—"

"Chris got shot," Filippo said.

"By who?" Mickey asked.

"My uncle Louie."

"*What?*"

"My fuckin' uncle Louie, my fuckin' uncle Louie, all right? What's wrong with you, you deaf?"

"What was your uncle doing in the house?"

"He stays over sometimes. I didn't think he'd be there tonight. I can't believe this shit fuckin' happened."

"And he shot Chris?"

"Yes, he shot Chris."

"What the hell're you talking about?"

"I was upstairs on the second floor," Filippo said. "I was in the study or wherever, where all my cousins' books are, and Chris was in the bedroom. I heard these shots—bang, bang. So I go in there. It's dark—I can see the guy's body, but I can't see his face. Then I see he's got a gun, so I . . . I fuckin' shot him. I just fuckin' shot him."

"*What?*" Mickey said. "You mean you killed your uncle?"

"I didn't know it was him."

"What the fuck are you talking about? You mean your uncle's body's in the house?"

"That's what I just told you."

"Jesus Christ," Mickey said.

"Jesus Christ," Filippo said, mimicking Mickey. "Why don't you shut up before I smack you? It's my uncle, not yours. I can't believe I shot him. I'm gonna go to hell for this."

Ralph made a sharp right, staying on Shore, and Chris's body fell onto Mickey again. Mickey shoved it away with so much force, Chris's head banged against the window on the opposite side of the car.

"Hey, take it easy back there," Ralph said.

"I still don't get it," Mickey said to Filippo. "How did Chris get shot?"

"My uncle shot him, you idiot," Filippo said.

"Why?"

"Why don't you go back and ask him?"

Mickey held his head in his hands and closed his eyes.

"So what're we gonna do now?" Mickey said. "When the cops find your uncle in the house they'll—"

"It don't matter," Filippo said. "So, there's a dead guy in the house. That has nothing to do with us."

"You ever heard of crime-scene investigators?" Mickey said. "They'll know Chris was there. They'll find his blood and try to match it—"

"Match it to what?" Filippo said. "They won't have Chris's body. Without his body they won't be able to tell nothing."

"But they'll have the other body," Mickey said.

"You love being stupid, don't you?" Filippo said.

Ralph pulled over near the docks on Sheepshead Bay. It wasn't far from where Chris and Mickey and Chris's father used to leave to go fishing all those mornings.

"All right," Ralph said to Filippo, "gimme the guns."

Filippo gave Ralph his gun, then Ralph said, "Where's Chris's?"

"I don't know," Filippo said. "I thought you had it."

"I don't have it," Ralph said.

"I gave it to you before we picked him up."

"You didn't give me shit."

"I took it off Chris," Filippo said. "I know I did."

"You left it in the house," Ralph said.

"I must've put it down when we were liftin' the body."

"Fuck," Ralph said, looking away. He waited a few seconds then said, "All right, maybe it don't matter. The gun's hot, anyway. Maybe it's better that way. The cops find a gun next to the guy's body—it'll throw 'em off track. They'll see the dead guy there and Chris's gun, and then they'll test the gun and find out it wasn't used to shoot the dead guy."

Ralph went outside and walked to the end of the dock. He tossed the two guns into the bay, then he came back into the car and drove away up Emmons Avenue. Looking out the window, Mickey remembered the time he caught that twenty-five-pound striped bass, posing with Chris and the fish afterward.

"Fuck," Ralph said, looking up into the rearview mirror.

Mickey turned around and saw the police car following directly behind them.

"Shit," Filippo said to Ralph. "You think he saw you on the dock?"

"It's all right," Ralph said, looking in the mirror. "He don't got the strobe light on—I don't think he's after us."

"What if they see the plates?" Mickey said.

"Don't matter," Ralph said. "The car's hot—I took it in Jersey this afternoon. They probably don't even got a report on it yet. Just keep cool—both of you. Mickey, make sure Chris is sitting up straight."

Mickey took a deep breath, then he straightened the body and held it in place, trying not to think about what he was doing. The police car followed them for another two blocks, then it turned left onto Ocean Avenue.

"That's it, they're gone," Ralph said.

"Jesus, I think I'm gonna have to change my underwear," Filippo said.

Mickey let go of Chris and shifted back away toward the window. Then he threw up onto his legs and onto the back of the front seat.

"What the fuck?" Filippo said.

The back of Mickey's throat was burning; he was about to throw up again.

"He blew fuckin' chunks," Filippo said to Ralph. "What'd I tell you? We shoulda brought my friend Jimmy tonight instead of this fuckin' faggot."

"Don't do that no more," Ralph said to Mickey.

Ralph turned onto Bedford Avenue and the car got quiet. Mickey opened the window a crack and the cool breeze helped relieve his nausea. He started thinking about Chris's mother, how she used to go on about Chris when Chris was a little kid—telling all the other mothers in the neighborhood how smart Chris was and how proud she was of him.

That was before Chris started getting into trouble, but even after that she always stood by him. She took good care of him, or tried to, anyway, after Chris's father took off. Even lately, when she was on the couch, getting drunk all the time, she never yelled at Chris or treated him badly.

On Avenue Z, Ralph pulled into a parking lot next to a closed hardware store. He drove to the back of the lot, where it was dark, and parked next to his beat-up Oldsmobile Omega.

"All right, first lemme take care of the body," Ralph said.

Ralph went out and opened the trunk of the Omega, then he came back to the stolen car and pulled Chris out. He lifted Chris up over his shoulder and put him inside the trunk of his car. Chris was small and fit inside easily.

Leaning inside the stolen car, Ralph said, "All right, both of you—get out of the car and take off all your clothes and put them inside your laundry bags."

"What for?" Mickey asked.

"Because you might have Chris's blood on them and I don't want his blood inside my car. Come on, just do it."

Mickey, Filippo and Ralph stood outside in the dark parking lot, and started getting undressed. Mickey took off his jacket and sweatshirt and felt the sting of the cold wind against his chest.

"Why are we putting the clothes in the laundry bags?" Mickey asked.

"So I can get rid of everything together," Ralph said.

"You mean you're not gonna try to sell the stuff we got?" Filippo said.

"That would be really bright," Ralph said. "With a dead

body in the house and another one in my trunk—this shit is way too hot."

"Yeah, and it don't matter," Filippo said. "I didn't find the ring, anyway. We probably only got a few hundred bucks here."

Ralph and Filippo had taken their shirts off, and they were taking off their pants. Mickey took out his wallet and keys, then he took off his pants, pulling each leg off over his shoes. He started shivering.

"Shoes too," Ralph said. "They coulda tracked blood. Come on, faster—we gotta get the fuck outta here."

Mickey took off his shoes and added them to the laundry bag.

"And don't forget the gloves," Ralph said.

Mickey added the dishwashing gloves and then tossed the laundry bag into the trunk, where Ralph and Filippo had already tossed their bags, on top of Chris's body.

"Okay, you two, wait in the car," Ralph said, "and I'll take care of the rest."

Wearing just socks and underwear, Mickey and Filippo got into Ralph's car—Mickey in the back and Filippo up front. Ralph, also in socks and underwear, took a wrench out of the trunk and returned to the stolen car. He kneeled down and started removing the hubcaps.

"What's he doing that for?" Mickey asked.

"Why do you think?" Filippo said. "He's makin' it look like the car was stolen for parts."

Ralph took off each hub cap and put them in the trunk of his car. Next, he opened the hood of the stolen car and took out the battery, then he went underneath and removed the muffler. Finally, he went inside the front of the car and, after a couple of minutes, came out with the car radio. He put all the parts in the trunk of the Omega with Chris's body. Still holding the wrench, Ralph returned to the stolen car and shattered the windshield in several places. Then he got into the Omega with Mickey and Filippo, put the wrench in the glove compartment, and drove away.

"So far so good," Ralph said as he turned back onto Avenue Z.

"So what are we gonna do now?" Mickey asked.

"*We* ain't gonna do nothin'," Ralph said. "I'm gonna drop off you and Filippo at home, and I'll take care of the rest."

"What do you mean?" Mickey said. "What're you gonna do with everything in the trunk? What're you gonna do with Chris?"

"Better you don't know," Ralph said. "That way, the police come talk to you, you got nothing to tell them. The only thing you gotta worry about is where you were tonight. I don't think the cops're gonna come talk to you—they should have no reason to—but if they do, what're you gonna say?"

"I don't know," Mickey said.

"Well you better think of something quick," Ralph said.

"I could say I was home," Mickey said.

"Who saw you there?" Ralph asked.

"Nobody," Mickey said.

"That's no good," Ralph said. "Somebody's gotta see you there or it's no good."

"I can say my father saw me," Mickey said. "He has Alzheimer's. He can't remember anything, anyway."

"That'll work," Ralph said. Then he said to Filippo, "What about you?"

"I was with you," Filippo said. "We were watching pornos."

"Okay, then that's the story, but we all gotta stick to it no matter what," Ralph said. "Mickey, check out the TV schedule when you get home, so if the cops ask, you can tell them all the shows you were watching. Filippo, what video were we watching?"

"*Flesh of the Lotus* with John Holmes as Johnny Wadd. I know all the scenes by heart."

"All right, then that's the story," Ralph said. "Me and Filippo was watching *Flesh of the Lotus*. The cops're gonna ask us all about Chris too. They'll say when's the last time we saw him, shit like that. When was the last time we saw Chris before tonight?"

"I saw him Thursday night," Mickey said. "After bowling."

"All right, so the cops ask, that's what you say. Me and Filippo saw him Thursday night, leaving the diner—eleven o'clock."

"What about Chris's mother?" Mickey asked.

"What about her?" Ralph said.

"Chris must've told her he was going someplace tonight. What if he told her he was meeting us?"

"Chris wasn't stupid," Ralph said. "He wouldn't tell his mother he was gonna rob a house."

"I know, but he could have told her he was doing something else with us," Mickey said, "like going bowling or something. Then if the cops ask us we'll have a different story."

"It still don't matter," Ralph said. "Maybe he told his mother he was gonna go out with us, what difference does it make? Maybe he was lying to his mother, maybe he wasn't really going to meet us. All we gotta say is we never saw Chris tonight. If we stick to that we'll be all right."

The car hit a pothole, and Chris's body and the rest of the stuff in the trunk banged around.

"So does anybody got any questions?" Ralph asked. "Everybody know exactly what they're gonna say?"

Mickey and Filippo said, "Yeah."

"Good," Ralph said. "And remember, the cops'll try tricks on you. They'll say one of us confessed so you might as well confess too, or they'll tell you some other BS. Whatever you do, don't talk—no matter what. If something goes wrong— if something happens and the cops find out that one of us was in that house—no squealing. If you go down, then you go down on your own and that's it. I'm telling you right now, if I take a murder rap because you ratted me out, I'll kill you. I don't care if I have to wait twenty years till I get out of jail, I'll still kill you. Remember that."

Ralph drove on and there was no more talking in the car until Ralph turned onto Albany Avenue and pulled into Mickey's driveway.

"Another thing," Ralph said to Mickey, "no talking to me or Filippo for at least a couple of months. We can't make it look like we're scared. Chris is probably gonna be reported missing in a day or two, and we gotta pretend like we're as surprised as everybody else. Right after the news about Chris breaks, I'm gonna drop us out of the bowling league. I'll tell the guy in charge we can't get a fourth guy to take

Chris's place. This way we don't have to see each other at all anymore. Got any questions?"

Mickey shook his head.

"Good, then go inside and get right to bed," Ralph said. "We gotta make this look good."

Mickey left the car and jogged up the driveway in his underwear and socks. When he entered the house and headed upstairs, Blackie started barking like crazy.

10

IT WAS FIVE in the morning and Mickey still couldn't fall asleep. Lying in bed, he kept seeing Chris's dead face in the ski mask, the blood dripping from his mouth.

Finally, he turned on the clock radio next to his bed to WINS all-news radio. There was no news about a robbery in Manhattan Beach and a dead body. Mickey was surprised because he'd thought the old man on the street would call the police right away.

Mickey spent a long time in the shower, staying under the hot water until the skin on his fingers wrinkled. After he got dressed, he listened to the news again in his room for a couple of hours, but there was still nothing about the robbery.

Mickey didn't feel like sitting through a Broadway show today, but he knew that staying home, waiting to hear something on the news would be torture. Besides, it would be good to see Rhonda again.

As Rhonda had promised, at eleven o'clock she was waiting on the corner of Bedford and J. She looked great in a
black miniskirt, black high heels, and a big red sweater
belted at the hips. Mickey, in jeans, sneakers, and a sweatshirt, felt underdressed.

When Rhonda got in Mickey kissed her on the lips, then
she ducked down under the dashboard and said, "Drive."

Mickey headed toward Ocean Avenue.

"My father went out and I'm afraid he's gonna come
back," she said. "Don't worry—I won't make you do this
again. I just need to break my father in slowly." Still bending
down, looking up at Mickey, she said, "So how are you?"

"Okay," Mickey said.

Mickey noticed Rhonda was wearing a different perfume
today. He didn't like it as much as the one she'd worn on
Friday.

"Is something wrong?" Rhonda asked.

"No," Mickey said. "Why?"

"You look kind of tired."

"I didn't get much sleep last night," Mickey said. "The
landlord's dog."

"Oh," Rhonda said. A few seconds later she added,
"You're not mad because I'm hiding from my father, are
you?"

"No, not at all."

Mickey turned right on Ocean Avenue and Rhonda sat up.

"I think we're safe now," she said. "Look what I have."

Rhonda reached into her pocketbook and took out a photograph, and Mickey glanced at it while he was driving. The
picture was from Ronny Feldman's birthday party. Mickey,

nine years old, with crooked bangs, was watching Ronny unwrap his presents. Rhonda was standing next to Mickey wearing a light blue party dress with white lace trim. Her face hadn't changed at all.

"Recognize me?" Rhonda asked.

"That's incredible," Mickey said, smiling.

"I wonder if we talked to each other."

"That would be funny."

"I think I remember you."

Mickey stopped smiling, seeing Ralph and Filippo carrying Chris's body down the staircase.

Putting the photograph away, Rhonda said, "So you excited about your first theater experience?"

"Yeah," Mickey said, still distracted.

"You really sound it."

"No, I am—really. I just didn't get a lot of sleep last night, like I told you."

Rhonda went on, talking about her favorite Broadway shows—*Pippin, A Chorus Line, Sweeney Todd.* Mickey was barely listening. Scenes from last night kept flashing in his head—Chris's body falling against him in the car, the old man screaming on the street, Ralph tossing the guns into Sheepshead Bay.

"What's that?" Mickey said, realizing that she had asked him a question.

"I asked you what your favorite movie of all time is," Rhonda said.

"Oh, *Star Wars,* I guess," Mickey said.

"That's *so* original," Rhonda said. "I like *Reds, Sophie's Choice,* and *Amadeus.* Did you see that?"

"What?" Mickey asked.

"*Amadeus.*"

"Nah," Mickey said.

Rhonda kept talking to Mickey about the movies and other things, but there were a lot of long silences too. Entering the Brooklyn-Queens Expressway, Rhonda said, "Oh my God, I know what's wrong."

She sounded like she really *knew.*

"This is the spot, isn't it?" she said. "The car accident your mother was in—you said it happened right here, on the Brooklyn-Queens Expressway. Did we just pass the spot or something?"

"Yeah," Mickey said, even though the accident had happened on a different part of the BQE, near the merger with the Gowanus Expressway.

During the rest of the trip into the city, they didn't talk much. They parked in a lot on Forty-eighth Street and walked down Ninth Avenue. Mickey didn't feel comfortable in this part of the city, especially with a girl. On every block there were porno theaters and sleazy-looking people hanging out in front of doorways and drugged-out homeless people asking for change. They passed a couple of Guardian Angels—Hispanic guys walking around in their red berets, looking tough, trying to protect the neighborhood—but Mickey still didn't feel safe and he held Rhonda's hand tightly.

Mickey asked Rhonda what kind of food she was in the mood for.

"Whatever," she said, looking away.

They went to an Italian restaurant on Restaurant Row. Lunch was going to cost at least thirty bucks and parking would cost around twenty. It would be no problem for today—Mickey had a hundred bucks with him—but he knew this would be the last time he'd be able to spend fifty or sixty bucks on a date. He remembered the Rolex from last night and he wished he'd kept it. He could have hocked it or sold it and used the money to pay off the rest of Angelo's debt and still had some left over.

Mickey ordered lasagna and Rhonda had a veal dish. As they ate, Rhonda did most of the talking. Mickey must have been staring off because Rhonda said, "Are you still upset about your mother?"

"No," Mickey said.

"Then is it something I did or said because—"

"No," Mickey said. "It's nothing."

"Well, you don't seem very happy to be with me today."

"Of course I'm happy," Mickey said. "I'm very happy."

During the rest of lunch, Mickey didn't say anything. He paid the bill, thirty-five bucks with tip, then they walked uptown a few blocks to the Winter Garden Theater on Fiftieth Street and Broadway.

The seats were great—in the middle section, three rows behind the orchestra. Waiting for the curtain to go up, Rhonda was still trying to talk to Mickey and Mickey was still quiet. He was worrying about what Ralph had done with Chris's body, and about Filippo's uncle's body, lying there in the house.

Mickey didn't pay much attention to the show. Rhonda

seemed to have a great time, though, smiling, singing along with the cast.

When they left the theater it was about five-thirty, and it was dark outside. They walked along Fiftieth Street toward Ninth Avenue. Rhonda was still singing one of the songs from the show, something about a cat named Skimble-shanks, and Mickey just wanted her to shut up.

On Ninth, Mickey noticed a tall, thin Puerto Rican guy standing in front of a bodega, looking at him and Rhonda as they passed by. Then, when they turned onto Forty-eighth Street, heading toward the parking lot, Mickey looked over his shoulder and noticed the guy following them.

"Come on, walk faster," Mickey whispered.

"Why?" Rhonda said in a normal tone of voice.

"Just do it," Mickey said.

Mickey and Rhonda walked faster, but Rhonda was on high heels and Mickey felt like he had to pull her along.

"I can't go this fast," Rhonda said. "What's wrong with you? Why're you pulling me?"

Mickey looked back and saw the guy behind them was also walking fast, gaining on them. But Mickey and Rhonda had reached the parking lot now, where the street was lit better, and there was a parking attendant sitting in a booth only a few feet away. The guy who'd been following them turned around and headed back toward Ninth Avenue.

Mickey paid the parking attendant then headed toward the car with Rhonda.

"What's wrong with you?" Rhonda said. "Why did you have to pull me like that?"

"That guy was following us," Mickey said.

"What guy?"

"The guy behind us. He followed us from that bodega."

"So why didn't you tell me?"

"I couldn't tell you."

"Then why'd you have to pull me? I almost twisted my ankle."

"Sorry," Mickey said, "I didn't have a choice. The guy would've mugged us."

They got in the car and drove out of the lot.

"You okay?" Mickey asked.

Rhonda didn't answer, her arms crossed in front of her chest. Mickey tried to hold her hand but she moved it away.

"Look, I didn't know what to do, all right?" Mickey said. "I really thought the guy wanted to mug us. You're lucky you didn't get your purse snatched."

"I really wish you'd tell me what's wrong," Rhonda said.

"Wrong with what?" Mickey said.

"Everything. You've been acting weird all day. You didn't talk at all during lunch, and you haven't said anything about the show."

"It was good," Mickey said.

"It was *good*? That's it? What was good about it? Did you like the singing, the dancing?"

"I liked all of it."

"It didn't seem like you liked any of it. You were just sitting there the whole time looking angry. Is it me? Did I do something wrong?"

"No, it's nothing, I told you. I had a great time today."

"Well, I didn't."

"I'm sorry to hear that."

"Sure you are."

They were driving down Eleventh Avenue and it was starting to drizzle. Mickey turned the wipers on with the slow setting. For a few minutes the only noise in the car was the occasional rubbing of the wipers against the windshield.

Finally, Mickey said, "Look, I really am sorry. I know I've been a little out of it today. But, believe me, it has nothing to do with you. I swear to God it doesn't."

"It's all right," Rhonda said quietly.

"No, it's not all right," Mickey said. "I've been acting like an idiot all day, but this isn't me. You know what I'm really like."

"Don't worry about it," Rhonda said. "It's not a big deal."

As they continued back to Brooklyn, Mickey tried to make conversation. He told Rhonda how much he liked the show and how he would love to go to another show with her sometime, but he couldn't keep his act up for long. Soon he started thinking about last night again and the dead silence returned.

Rhonda asked Mickey to drop her off at the corner of her block, instead of in front of her house, so her father wouldn't see. Mickey pulled into a parking spot on the corner of Avenue I and East Twenty-third Street and put the car in park.

"Let me take you out to dinner one night this week," Mickey said. "How about Wednesday night?"

"Maybe," Rhonda said.

"Maybe?"

"I don't know what night's good for me."

"I'll call you."

Mickey was trying to look into Rhonda's eyes, but she was looking away, fidgeting with the door handle. Mickey leaned around and kissed her, but it wasn't anything like the kiss the other night. She didn't open her mouth and she pulled back quickly and said, "Good night, Mickey." Then she left the car and headed up the block toward her house without even looking back or waving.

Mickey drove away, hating himself for ruining everything, for acting like such a jerk, then he turned onto Albany Avenue and saw the police car parked in front of his house and the two officers out front talking to his neighbors.

11

MICKEY PARKED ACROSS the street from his house and got out of his car slowly. The neighbors noticed him and stopped talking to the officers and to each other right away. Mickey's landlord Joseph was there, and so was Shawn, the thirteen-year-old kid from next door, and Shawn's parents, and John Finley and his wife Kathy, and Kenny Dugan from up the street. Then Mickey saw Mrs. Turner, Chris's mother, standing off to the side by the driveway. Everyone was looking at Mickey with sad, disappointed expressions, probably wondering how a kid like Mickey, who'd always seemed like he'd had such a good head on his shoulders and was going to go places in life, had wound up getting involved in something like this.

The two officers saw Mickey and immediately stopped what they were doing and walked toward him, looking very serious, to head him off before he reached the house. Mickey expected to be thrown back against the car and handcuffed from behind and the officers to start reading him his rights.

"You Mickey Prada?" one of the officers asked. He was a stocky guy with a thick brown mustache.

"Yeah," Mickey said, bracing himself.

"I'm afraid I have some bad news for you," the officer said. "Your father was killed this afternoon."

"What did you just say?" Mickey said.

"I said your father was killed this afternoon," the officer said. "He was struck by a car while crossing Fort Hamilton Parkway. We're very sorry."

It seemed like a second later Mickey was sitting on his stoop, the two officers standing in front of him, and he had no idea how he got there. The other officer, who was tall with a short blond crew cut, was explaining how the accident had happened. Sal Prada had been trying to cross Fort Hamilton Parkway against the light at approximately three-thirty P.M. when a laundry truck slammed into him. Mickey was barely paying attention, but he heard the officer say "your father died instantly" and "he didn't feel any pain."

The neighbors came over to Mickey, one by one, trying to console him. Chris's mother sat next to Mickey on the stoop and put an arm around him. Mickey could smell alcohol on her breath as she said, "Don't worry, your father's in heaven now and he's not suffering anymore." She kissed Mickey on the cheek and then said, "I know this is a terrible time for you, but do you got any idea where Chris is?"

Mickey looked at the officers standing nearby, only a few feet away. But the officers were busy, writing in their pads, and didn't seem to be eavesdropping.

"What do you mean?" Mickey asked.

"He didn't come home last night and I haven't heard from

him all day," Mrs. Turner said. "I thought he might've gone to Atlantic City or something with you and maybe he didn't tell me."

"I haven't seen him since last Thursday night," Mickey said.

"I'm sure he'll come home soon," Mrs. Turner said. "And when he does I'll tell him to come over and be with you."

After a few minutes of consoling Mickey, Mrs. Turner returned to her house across the street. The police officer with the mustache gave Mickey some personal items that were found on Sal—his wallet and keys—and explained that the body was currently in the Victory Memorial Hospital morgue.

"If you want to come with us to ID the body, we'd be glad to give you a lift."

Mickey nodded and followed the officers to the squad car. During the twenty-or-so-minute drive to Bay Ridge, Mickey stared out the window while the officers up front bullshitted about baseball.

At the hospital, Mickey was led down to the morgue. An attendant explained that the body was in "bad shape," so instead of showing Mickey the actual body, he showed him a black-and-white photograph—a side view of Sal Prada's face. Mickey recognized his father immediately and the attendant asked him to sign the picture.

Mickey was given a card with a number to call to give instructions on where to send the body, then the officers led Mickey back upstairs.

In the hospital's lobby, the blond officer said to Mickey, "We understand that your father was suffering from Alzheimer's disease and had also recently suffered a stroke. Is that correct?"

"Yes," Mickey said.

"Do you have any idea why he was in the Fort Hamilton Parkway vicinity today?" the officer asked.

"No," Mickey said. "Not really. I mean this is the neighborhood where he grew up, Bay Ridge, and he sometimes got confused about the past."

"We also understand this wasn't the first time your father wandered away," the officer said.

"No it wasn't," Mickey said.

"Excuse me for saying this, but if this happened before, why wasn't your father receiving supervision?"

"You mean why wasn't he in a home?" Mickey asked.

"Yes. Or why—"

"Because I didn't want to put him in a home, all right? I wanted to take care of him. Would you put your father away in a nursing home?"

"I don't know, but if I didn't put him away I probably wouldn't let him wander the streets, either."

Mickey was about to tell the blond officer to go fuck himself when the officer with the mustache cut in and said to his partner, "I think we should get going now."

They drove Mickey back to his house. Mickey got out of the car without saying anything, letting the door slam behind him.

All the commotion in front of the house had cleared, and Mickey went up to his apartment. He sat at the kitchen table, looking through Sal Prada's old address book. Most of the names in the book were of old friends of his father's who had died or whom his father had fallen out of touch with.

But Mickey called all the people he thought would want to hear about his father's death, including his father's cousin Carmine on Staten Island. Carmine was in his eighties and couldn't hear very well. Mickey had to keep yelling, "My father died!" until Carmine finally understood. "Oh," Carmine said, not sounding very surprised or upset. Mickey explained how his father had died and Carmine said, "Oh, that's too bad."

Mickey called a few other distant relatives and old friends of his father and got similar reactions. No one seemed very surprised to hear that Sal Prada was dead, and they didn't seem to care very much, either.

When he finished calling, Mickey went into his room and turned on the radio. He listened for an entire hour, lying in bed, but there was still nothing about a robbery or a murder in Manhattan Beach.

Downstairs, in his landlord's apartment, Blackie was barking as loudly as usual; otherwise, the apartment was quiet and suddenly seemed very empty.

It was after eleven, but Mickey decided to call Rhonda, anyway. A woman answered the phone—it sounded like her stepmother—and Mickey asked to speak with Rhonda. About a minute went by and then Rhonda picked up.

"Rhonda, it's Mickey."

There was a long pause then she said, "Hi."

"Sorry to call so late," Mickey said.

"It's okay," she said. "So what do you want?"

"My father died today."

Rhonda hesitated then said, "Are you serious? What happened?"

Mickey explained.

"My God, that's so awful," Rhonda said. "I'm so sorry."

"So what're you doing right now?" Mickey asked.

"Now?"

"Yeah. You feel like going to a diner and getting some dessert or coffee or something? I mean I know it's short notice but I really want to see you again and—"

"I can't now," Rhonda said. "I mean it's late and I have an early class tomorrow and—"

"Oh," Mickey said, "because I really wanted to make up for today. I know I was an asshole."

"I'm sorry," Rhonda said. "I can't."

"It's okay," Mickey said. "We'll do it some other time then."

"Yeah, some other time," Rhonda said. "I'm really sorry about your father."

"Thanks," Mickey said.

He wanted to say something else but Rhonda said, "Bye, Mickey," and hung up quickly.

AT EIGHT THE next morning, Mickey called Harry at home and explained he would have to take the morning off.

"You better have a good reason," Harry said.

"My father died," Mickey said.

"Oh, shit, I'm sorry," Harry said, for once in his life sounding sincere. He asked Mickey how it happened and after Mickey told him he said, "You sure you don't wanna take the whole day?"

"Nah, just the morning," Mickey said. "I'll see you at noon."

Mickey spent most of the morning on the phone. He

looked in the yellow pages for funeral homes and called a few that didn't seem too expensive. But even the cheapest funeral would cost three thousand bucks, not including the price of the coffin, the hearse, or the cemetery plot. Mickey only had about nine hundred left in the bank and he still owed Artie over a thousand, so there was no way he could even afford a coffin.

Mickey decided to forget the funeral. He would just have a wake for his father and have the body cremated. He found a wake/cremation package for twenty-two hundred bucks at a funeral home on Avenue U. When Mickey explained his financial situation, the funeral director agreed to let him pay with an interest-free payment plan—two hundred bucks up front, and then payments of at least a hundred a month.

After Mickey called the morgue and arranged for the body to be delivered to the funeral home, he called a few of his father's relatives and old friends and told them about the wake on Wednesday. He even called Artie, leaving a message with his wife, then he called up some of the neighbors who had been by the house yesterday. He called Chris's mother last. She said she wanted to come, but she was too worried about Chris to think about anything else. Mickey said he understood.

"I haven't seen him in two days now, and it's just not like him not to call," she said.

"Like I told you," Mickey said, "I haven't seen him since Thursday night."

"He left to go out Saturday night," Mrs. Turner said. "I heard the door slam, but he didn't say where he was going.

I was drinkin' a little bit that night, so maybe he said something and I didn't hear him."

"I'm sure he's all right," Mickey said.

"If I don't hear something by noon, I'm calling the police," Mrs. Turner said. "This just isn't like Chris."

When Mickey got off the phone he was sweating all over. He showered and dressed for work, leaving his apartment at a quarter to twelve. At the grocery store on Avenue J, he bought a copy of the *Daily News* and flipped through it as he walked, but there was nothing about the robbery.

At work, five or six customers were on line, waiting to order from Harry and Charlie.

"Hey, Mickey," Charlie said, stopping what he was doing. "I heard about your father. Man, I'm really sorry."

"It's all right," Mickey said.

"If there's anything I can do, you just lemme know and I'll be there for you, all right?"

"Yeah," Mickey said.

Mickey went to the back of the store and immediately bent over the sink and splashed his face with cold water. Then he put on his apron and returned to the front of the store. Around one, the lunch crowd thinned out and Harry left for the afternoon.

"Thank *God,*" Charlie said to Mickey when the door closed behind Harry. "Being trapped here with that asshole all morning was like being in hell. You shoulda seen him— runnin' me around, givin' me orders. I'm busy cutting a piece of salmon for this one lady when he tells me to take this guy's order. I say to him, 'I only got two hands,' and he goes, 'Talk back to me again like that and you're fired.' Said it right there, right in front of everybody. Swear to God, I almost quit on his ass right then. Shoulda done it too—worth it not to see his fat, wrinkly-ass face no more."

"You get AM stations on that?" Mickey said, motioning with his chin toward Charlie's boom box in the corner.

"Yeah," Charlie said. "What you lookin' for, sports scores?"

"Yeah," Mickey lied. "You mind?"

"Go ahead."

Mickey turned on the boom box and started searching for a news station.

"So Harry told me some about what happened," Charlie said. "Your father had Alzheimer's, huh?"

"How'd you know?" Mickey asked. He had never talked to Charlie about his father.

"Harry told me," Charlie said.

"Oh," Mickey said, finding the station he'd been looking for.

"Yeah, my old man died when I was ten," Charlie said. "Heart attack."

"Sorry," Mickey said, distracted by a story on the news, but it was about a murder in the Bronx, not Brooklyn.

"So you gotta let me know when the funeral is, and I'll be there," Charlie said.

"There won't be a funeral, just a wake," Mickey said.

"Whatever," Charlie said. "I'll be there for you."

The bell above the door rang then Mickey, still kneeling by the boom box, heard Rhonda say, "Is Mickey in today?"

Mickey stood up, suddenly smiling widely, and saw Rhonda standing on the other side of the counter. She was wearing jeans and a dungaree jacket, a knapsack slung over one shoulder.

"Mickey," Rhonda said, looking surprised. "You're here."

Mickey took off his apron, tossed it behind him on the counter, and went around the fish stands to greet her. He tried to kiss her but she pulled away.

"I have a class in a half hour," she said. "I just came by to drop off a card. I didn't think you'd even be here today."

Rhonda took out an envelope from her jacket pocket and handed it to Mickey.

"Thanks," Mickey said, suddenly happier than he'd been in days. "So how're you doing? You look great."

"Thanks," Rhonda said quickly. "Anyway, I just wanted to give you the card and tell you how sorry I am."

"It's all right," Mickey said. "He was old and I guess it was just his time."

"I thought you said he was hit by a car."

"He was. Hey, you wanna go get some lunch with me? I haven't had anything to eat all day."

"I'd like to," Rhonda said, "but I really have to get to my class."

"You said it doesn't start for a half hour. We could just go to the pizza place across the street and—"

"No, I really can't. Sorry. I mean I have to walk to school and—"

"Can I walk you?"

"That's okay," Rhonda said. "I mean I have to stop home first and get some books and—"

"You don't have your books in your bag?"

Rhonda hesitated then said, "These were for my morning

classes." She looked at her watch. "Actually, I should probably leave right now."

"Hey, you want to go to a movie Friday night?" Mickey
asked.

"I can't," Rhonda said.

"Then how about Saturday?"

"I don't know," Rhonda said, taking a step toward the door.

"Will you come to my father's wake?" Mickey asked.

"When is it?"

"Wednesday at ten."

"I have a class Wednesday at eleven."

"A wake lasts all day," Mickey said. "Maybe you can come
after your class, in the afternoon—"

"Maybe," Rhonda said.

"Is something wrong?" Mickey asked.

"No," Rhonda said. "I'm just in a hurry."

Mickey wrote down the address of the wake on a Vincent's Fish Market business card and handed it to Rhonda.

"You sure something isn't wrong?" Mickey said.

"Positive," Rhonda said. "I just can't talk right now."

"Okay," Mickey said. "I hope I see you at the wake."

When Rhonda was gone, Mickey opened the card and
read the printed message which began, *Words alone cannot
relieve the sorrow you must feel right now.*

MICKEY LEFT WORK early to make it home in time to watch the
six o'clock news, but there was still no mention of the robbery and murder. He fried up some shrimp and scallops that
he'd brought home, added Minute Rice, and stirred it all

together. He had a few bites, but he wasn't really hungry. He put away the leftovers in the fridge and opened the card Rhonda had given him for what must have been the twentieth time. The card was signed "Rhonda," not "Love, Rhonda," and he hoped this wasn't a bad sign.

Later, Mickey called Chris's mother, figuring it would look suspicious if he didn't keep in touch.

"Mickey, I'll have to call you back—the police just walked in."

On the word "police" a jolt went through Mickey's chest, but he managed to catch his breath quickly. "What happened?"

"I'll call you back later, okay?" Mrs. Turner said.

After Mickey hung up he looked out his bedroom window and saw the police car parked in front of Mrs. Turner's house. To keep busy, he started cleaning out his father's room. He got a few Hefty bags from the kitchen, then he filled the bags with old clothes from the dresser drawers and the closet, coughing from the smell of mothballs. His father had had most of these clothes for as long as Mickey could remember. An ugly plaid jacket reminded him of being at the racetrack with his father years ago, standing in front of the betting windows, while his father read the *Racing Form*. Mickey put the jacket up to his nose, not surprised that it still smelled faintly of cigarette smoke.

Mickey planned to bring the stuff to the Salvation Army, and if they didn't want it he'd just dump it on the street. He filled six bags with clothes and was starting to clean out the papers and other junk from the drawers of his father's dresser when the doorbell rang. Terrified, imagining the police had connected him to Chris's disappearance, Mickey went across the apartment to his room and looked out the window. He was relieved to see that the police car was gone. The doorbell rang again. As he headed down the stairs to answer it, Mickey called out, "One sec, I'm coming."

He opened the door and saw Mrs. Turner standing there crying into a bunch of crumpled napkins.

"What's wrong?" Mickey asked. "What's going on?"

Mrs. Turner continued to cry for a few seconds, unable to speak, then she said, "He's dead. I know he's dead."

"What do you mean?" Mickey said. "How do you know that? Is that what the police told you?"

"No, but I just know it," she said. "He's not coming back. He's gone, Mickey. Gone forever."

She hugged Mickey, crying with her chin on his shoulder.

"It isn't fair," she said. "Why did this have to happen to him? He was a good kid. He was trying to get his life together."

"You don't know anything happened," Mickey said.

"I know," she said. "He wouldn't just leave for somewhere without calling. The police say there's still a chance, they'll look for him, but I know he's gone. I just know it."

Mrs. Turner stayed with Mickey for a while longer, crying, and Mickey kept telling her, "Don't worry, they'll find him," and "I'm sure he's fine," and anything else he could think of to make her feel better.

Finally, Mrs. Turner said she would let Mickey know if there was any news, and then she walked away. Mickey watched her cross the street with her shoulders slumped and the wet napkins still in her hand.

12

Five ten o'clock news, the story about the Manhattan Beach robbery finally broke. A reporter live on the scene in front of the house on Hastings Street said that the police were trying to solve a bizarre mystery. The reporter explained how Robert and Barbara Rosselli had returned home from their vacation home in Pocono Pines, Pennsylvania, late last night when they discovered that their house had been robbed. The Rossellis had discovered blood on the floor in their bedroom, as well as a small handgun.

As the reporter spoke, footage of the outside of the house taken earlier in the day was shown. Then Mr. Rosselli came on, looking scared, saying pretty much what the reporter had said. A neighbor of the Rossellis said that he was shocked that something like this had happened in Manhattan Beach because it was such a calm, friendly neighborhood. The reporter returned live outside the house and said that the police were currently analyzing the blood and trying to trace the gun, but that they had no leads in the case.

Mickey watched the report, mesmerized, waiting for a mention of Filippo's uncle Louie, but the mention never came. When the report ended, Mickey turned to the Channel Eleven news to see if he could find out any more information. He watched for about fifteen minutes, until the sports came on, but there was nothing about the robbery.

Mickey couldn't believe he had been so stupid. He picked up the phone then realized he didn't know Filippo's or Ralph's phone numbers. He knew Filippo's last name—Castellano—but instead of calling Information for the number, he decided to go talk to him in person.

Without bothering to put on a jacket, Mickey walked a few blocks to Filippo's house on East Forty-third Street. Mickey passed by the semi-attached, two-family brick house all the time, but he had never been inside.

After ringing the bell, Mickey heard heavy footsteps and then Filippo's father opened the door. Mickey had seen Mr. Castellano around the neighborhood for years, but they had never spoken. He was a big fat guy with gray streaks in his black hair, and he had a thick mostly gray mustache. Chris had told Mickey that Mr. Castellano was a garbageman and he used to hit Filippo, but that was about all Mickey knew about him.

"Is Filippo here?" Mickey asked.

"Who are you?"

Mickey was surprised Mr. Castellano didn't at least recognize him.

"Mickey. I'm on a bowling team with Filippo."

"He ain't here."

"When will he be home?"

"Who the fuck knows?"

As Mickey said, "Thanks," the door slammed. Mickey was heading home when he had an idea where Filippo could be. The Knights of Columbus had a club on Avenue J, and Filippo sometimes hung out there, drinking and playing pool. When Mickey entered the dank, dimly lit club, he spotted Filippo sitting at the bar, talking to the bartender. Filippo saw Mickey, got off his bar stool, and came over to meet him by the door.

"What the hell're you doing here?" Filippo said.

"You fuckin' lied to me," Mickey said.

Filippo leaned close to Mickey's ear and whispered, "Outside," then he left the club ahead of Mickey. When Mickey met Filippo on the sidewalk, Filippo said, "You fuckin' takin' stupid pills or something? We're not supposed to see each other."

"Your uncle wasn't in that house," Mickey said.

"What the fuck're you talkin' about?"

"I just watched the news. The cops found the blood and the gun, but they didn't find a body."

"Will you shut the fuck . . . ?" Filippo looked around. An old guy was walking his dog across the street, but he wasn't paying attention.

"Did you kill Chris?" Mickey asked.

"*What?*" Filippo said. "You tryin' to get your ass kicked?"

"It was either you or Ralph because there wasn't anybody else in the house."

"Maybe the cops didn't find my uncle's body yet."

"Tell me what happened or I'm going to the cops right now."

"You're not that stupid," Filippo said. "You robbed that house too. You go to the cops you're turnin' yourself in."

"I don't give a shit," Mickey said. "I want to know what happened."

Filippo looked at the guy walking his dog across the street and said to Mickey, "Come on." Filippo and Mickey walked farther up the block and stopped near the corner where no one was around.

"All right, I'll tell you the truth," Filippo said, "but you gotta swear to me you won't go to the cops."

"Just tell me," Mickey said.

Filippo shook his head and covered his face with his hands. He started crying. He turned away from Mickey and said, "I did it, but it was an accident, I swear to God. My gun just went off."

Filippo continued crying, wiping his cheeks.

"What do you mean, an accident?" Mickey said. "How could it've been an accident?"

"We were in my cousin's bedroom," Filippo said. "I thought I heard something near the bathroom. I said, 'Chris, is that you?' But he didn't answer—probably Chris just fucking around, you know? So I just panicked and . . . I don't even remember what happened, it happened so fast. I didn't wanna fuckin' kill him. He was my friend."

Filippo rubbed his eyes with the backs of his hands.

"Why were there two shots?" Mickey said.

"I shot him twice," Filippo said. "It was just like a reflex—I couldn't stop my finger. You gotta believe me. Why would I want to hurt Chris? I loved the fuckin' guy."

Mickey looked up at the dark sky, not sure how he felt. He hated Filippo, but he also felt sorry for him.

"Why'd you lie?" Mickey asked.

"I don't know," Filippo said. "I just wasn't thinking straight, I guess—it all happened so fast. One second everything was all right, the next second Chris was dead. And I was scared of Ralph. He's killed people before. Just last year he shot a nigger and a chink on the Island—they never caught him for it. Anyway, that's the truth, but you can't go to the cops. You were robbing the house too—you helped us take the body out. You call the cops, we all go to jail."

Mickey knew Filippo was right; like it or not, he was involved.

"So what the hell're you gonna tell Ralph?" Mickey said.

"I'll take care of it," Filippo said. "Ralph's my friend. I'll make him understand."

Mickey remembered Mrs. Turner, crying into the ball of napkins. He didn't know how he'd be able to face her again.

"I guess we have no choice now," Mickey said. "I've gotta go home."

As Mickey started away, Filippo said, "Hey, Mickey."

Mickey turned around.

"Sorry."

Mickey realized tonight was the first time Filippo had ever talked to him normally, without acting like an asshole. Mickey walked away without saying anything.

13

WHEN MICKEY ENTERED his apartment, he fell to his knees and broke down crying. He hadn't cried at all about Chris or his father, and it all hit him at once. For about half an hour, he remained on the floor, sobbing uncontrollably. Finally, he stood up, feeling exhausted, and he didn't know how he'd make it through the next few days.

At work the next day, Mickey felt out of it, as if he had a bad hangover. He kept thinking about Chris, bleeding to death on the bedroom floor, and felt like it was his fault. He knew this was crazy, that he'd had nothing to do with what had happened, but he couldn't stop feeling responsible.

On his way home, Mickey walked quickly along Albany Avenue, afraid Mrs. Turner would see him and come out to talk to him. As he turned into his driveway, Mickey glanced across the street at Mrs. Turner's house and saw that the downstairs lights were on. He pictured her sprawled out on the couch, drinking.

Mickey spent the evening making last-minute calls to old friends of his father, telling them about the wake tomorrow. He'd been missing Rhonda all day and he called her, leaving a message on her answering machine, reminding her to stop by tomorrow if she could. At ten o'clock, he didn't bother watching the news, afraid he'd find out that Chris's body had been discovered, or that the old man on the street had come forward.

At around nine-thirty on Wednesday morning, Mickey arrived at the Sabatino Funeral Home on Avenue U wearing his best black pants and a brown shirt that he'd had since his first year of high school. The funeral director told him how sorry he was about his loss, and then he led him to a room where Sal Prada's body was in a casket. The funeral director sat with him for a while on the pew near the casket and then left him alone.

About twenty minutes later, cousin Carmine arrived with an old woman Mickey had never met. Carmine was hunched over and frail and didn't recognize Mickey. After Carmine and the old woman sat down in the pew in front of Mickey, Mickey leaned forward and said, "Carmine," a few times until he finally heard him and turned around.

"It's me—Mickey."

Carmine continued to squint for a few seconds, then said, "Mickey, shit, I didn't recognize you."

Mickey and Carmine shook hands, then Carmine introduced Mickey to the woman, his "girlfriend Ruth," who must have been about ninety.

"Hey, I'm sorry about your father," Carmine said, "but he

was a good guy. Yeah, he was a good guy." He started squinting again. "Now I know what's different about you—it's your
nose. It grew, didn't it?"

"Yeah, a little," Mickey said, remembering why he'd never
liked Carmine.

"A little?" Carmine said. "You kiddin' me? You look like
the spittin' image of your father now. See that Ruth? That's
Sal's nose."

Carmine and Ruth stayed for about an hour, and Mickey
wished they'd left sooner.

The rest of the morning no one else showed up. Mrs.
Turner was probably too worried about Chris, and some of
the people Mickey had called were too old and sick to
travel. Tomorrow was Thanksgiving Day and some people
might have left town early. Still, Mickey expected at least a
couple of Sal's old friends from work to come, and he was
especially hoping to see Rhonda.

The funeral director returned to the room and offered to
get Mickey something to eat for lunch, but Mickey said he
wasn't hungry. Then, about half an hour later, Charlie
arrived, wearing a black suit and a tie.

"Guess I'm early," Charlie said, sitting down next to
Mickey.

"Hey, how's it going?" Mickey said, smiling. "Thanks for
coming."

"What did you think, I'm not gonna show up to your
father's wake? Where's your girlfriend at?"

"She was here before," Mickey lied. "She might stop by
again later."

"That's cool," Charlie said. "I only came here for you. I

thought I was gonna get my ass jumped in this neighborhood."

"It's during the day," Mickey said.

"You wanna come hang out in Bed Sty during the day?" Charlie said. "But it don't matter—I got protection now." He looked around. "I know this ain't exactly the time and place, but feel this right here."

Charlie patted the front of his suit near his chest. Mickey touched the area, making out the shape of a gun in the inside pocket.

"Jesus," Mickey said.

"Thirty-eight Special, shoots six rounds," Charlie said. "My friend Andre got it for me on the street."

"You don't want to carry that around with you," Mickey said.

"Really," Charlie said. "Why don't I?"

"You just don't," Mickey said.

"What do I look like, I'm five years old?" Charlie said. "You don't gotta worry about me, daddy, I'll be a good boy. I won't go play cowboys and Indians with my friends." Charlie laughed. "Don't worry, I'm not planning to *use* it. It's just for protection—so if shit goes down like what went down that night, I can defend myself."

"Just be careful," Mickey said.

"I will, daddy, I will," Charlie said. He looked around. "So you gonna have some more family coming later on?"

"We don't really have a very big family," Mickey said.

"That's cool," Charlie said. "My family's not big, either. Got my mother and brothers and a couple aunts and uncles, but that's it. So how old was your father, anyway?"

"Seventy-five," Mickey said.

Charlie rested a hand on Mickey's shoulder.

"You believe in God?" Charlie asked.

The question surprised Mickey.

"I don't know," Mickey said.

"What do you mean, you don't know?" Charlie said. "There're only two answers, yes or no."

Thinking about everything that had happened to him lately, Mickey said, "No. I guess I don't."

"What about your father?" Charlie asked.

"Yeah, right," Mickey said. "He used to go to Atlantic City on Easter Sunday."

"It don't matter," Charlie said, "because your father's in heaven right now. I know a lot of people don't believe in the Lord Almighty, but all that means is there a lot of surprised dead people."

Mickey smiled even though he didn't want to.

Charlie left at around two and no one else came the rest of the day. When Mickey came home he called Rhonda and left a message with her stepmother. He spent the rest of the evening rehearsing what he would say when she called back, but the phone never rang.

AT TEN O'CLOCK the next morning, Thanksgiving Day, Mickey picked up his father's ashes from the funeral home and headed straight to Aqueduct Racetrack in Queens, where there was an early holiday racing card. Instead of parking in the street outside the track where he used to park with his father, he paid the buck fifty and parked in the track's parking lot. It was chilly and windy and there wasn't much sun. With the canister of ashes tucked under his coat, Mickey paid for his general admission and went into the grandstand.

It was early, about forty-five minutes to post time for the first race. Mickey walked straight past the TV monitors where he used to watch the races with his father on cold winter days, and back outside to the front of the grandstand. Wanting to get this over with, he kept walking, past the paddock, toward the rail.

Opening the canister with his father's ashes, Mickey remembered when he was eight years old and he'd begged his father to buy him a pet cat. Finally, one afternoon after school, Sal Prada took Mickey to a pet store on Avenue N and Mickey picked out a Tabby. Mickey named the kitten Spunky. Mickey played with Spunky all the time and he took good care of him. He always made sure there was fresh food and water in Spunky's dishes, and he changed his litter box two times a week.

But Spunky had a problem. He'd been taken away from his mother too soon and he only used his litter box once in a while. One night, when Sal was barefoot and on his way to the bathroom, he stepped on a piece of Spunky's shit. Sal started screaming at Mickey and the cat, and he told Mickey that if Spunky didn't learn how to use his litter box they were going to get rid of him. For the next few weeks, Mickey raced home every day after school and searched the entire apartment, making sure Spunky had used his litter box. But one night Sal started screaming, "That's it! Where is he? Where's that fuckin' animal?"

Sal barged into Mickey's room and found Spunky next to Mickey in Mickey's bed. Sal lifted the screeching cat up by his tail.

"What the hell are you doing?" Mickey said. "What's wrong with you?"

"The fuckin' cat shit in my bed," Sal said. "I warned you, I fuckin' warned you! That stupid animal's outta here . . . for good!"

Sal carried Spunky by his tail into the kitchen and put him in a shopping bag, rolling up the bag so that the cat couldn't get out.

"Let him go!" Mickey screamed. "Let him go!"

Sal pushed past Mickey and left the apartment. Mickey, barefoot and screaming, ran after his father, but Sal kept pushing Mickey away. Sal got into his car and pulled out of the driveway. Mickey chased the car halfway up the block then collapsed onto the street, crying hysterically.

About half an hour later, Sal Prada returned home without Spunky.

"Where is he?!" Mickey screamed. "What did you do with him?!"

Sal went into his room and locked the door. Mickey banged on the door all night, finally falling asleep in the hallway.

The next day, Mickey demanded to know what happened to Spunky but Sal just said, "Forget about him, he's gone." Mickey kept screaming and crying until Sal finally said, "All right, you wanna know where your fuckin' cat is? I tossed him out the window on the Belt Parkway. Trust me, you'll never see that stinkin' animal again."

Leaning over the rail, Mickey cocked his arm back and flung his father's ashes toward the racetrack. A strong wind blew most of the ashes back toward him. Seagulls swooped down toward the concrete, thinking someone was feeding them bread crumbs, then took off quickly when they realized their mistake.

Mickey tossed the canister into a garbage can and headed back toward the grandstand with his hands deep in his pockets and his head down against the wind.

14

ON HIS WAY home from the racetrack, Mickey stopped at the White Castle near Starrett City and bought a dozen mini-cheeseburgers and a few orders of fries. He took the food to go and ate on the floor in his room, watching the Thanksgiving Day football games.

Except for the meal, it wasn't much different from Mickey's usual Thanksgivings. He and his father used to cook a small turkey or buy some presliced white meat and a few legs from the supermarket deli counter. They would also buy cans of sweet potatoes and cranberry sauce and a box of powdered mashed potatoes. Mickey would fix himself a plate of food then go into his room to watch football.

Last Thanksgiving, after the football games, Mickey had gone to see a James Bond movie with Chris. Mickey didn't feel like going to the movies by himself tonight, and he had nothing else to do. He figured his friends from high school were home for the holiday, but they were probably busy with their families. Besides, no one had tried to get in touch with him.

Mickey decided to take a drive, just to get out of the apartment and clear his head. It was only seven o'clock but the Brooklyn streets were dark and empty. The only stores open were a few newsstands and all-night grocery stores. Mickey turned on the radio to kill the silence in the car, then he got tired of listening and turned it off.

Mickey made a left off of Flatlands Avenue onto Avenue I. He drove past Albany Avenue and continued along I to East Twenty-third Street—Rhonda's block. He parked across the street from her house and got out. There were lights on in most of the rooms, and as Mickey walked closer he could hear people laughing inside. He walked up the driveway and looked in through a window. About ten people, including Rhonda, were seated at a long table. Mickey couldn't understand why she hadn't invited him to dinner tonight. She knew his father had died and that he probably didn't have anyplace else to go. He wondered if he had said something to upset her.

For about ten minutes, maybe longer, Mickey stood in the driveway, looking in the window, then he returned to his car and drove home.

In front of the open refrigerator, he ate leftover cheese-burgers, getting angrier at Rhonda with each bite. Finally, he couldn't take it anymore. He picked up the phone in the kitchen and dialed her number.

"Hello," her father said.

Mickey was silent.

"Hello," her father said louder.

Mickey held the receiver up to his ear for a few more seconds, then he hung up. He grabbed a plate from the dish rack and smashed it on the floor.

MICKEY TRANSFERRED THE fresh lobsters from the crates to the tanks, then he got to work gutting the tuna and cutting them into steaks. It was good to be busy, to forget about the rest of his life for a while.

In the middle of the afternoon, Mickey took a break, sitting on a stool in the corner, drinking a Pepsi and looking through the *Daily News*. There was nothing about Chris or the robbery. He looked up from the newspaper and watched Charlie making change for an old man at the register. The man handed Charlie a bill and then Charlie opened the register and gave the man his change and said, "Thank you." The man left the store and Charlie closed the register without putting the twenty inside.

Charlie walked behind the fish stands, his hands disappearing out of view, then he came around to where Mickey was sitting.

"Damn, it's been a long day," Charlie said. "Sometimes I think time moves slower in this store, like we're in the *Twilight Zone* or something. I gotta put on some tunes to keep me awake."

Charlie knelt down to his boom box and a few seconds later rap music started blasting. Charlie started nodding his head to the beat of the music as he cleaned the countertop.

Mickey didn't know what to do. He really didn't care if

Charlie was stealing from Harry—let him take all of Harry's money if he wanted to—but he didn't want to see him get caught.

Mickey went over to where Charlie was working. Charlie looked up at him, still bobbing his head to the music and said, "What's the matter, don't like my man Kurtis Blow?"

"I saw you," Mickey said.

Charlie turned away, looking down at the counter he was cleaning.

After a few seconds of silence, Charlie said, "Saw me what?"

"I saw you take that money," Mickey said. "You never put it in the register."

"I did too put it in the register."

"I was watching," Mickey said. "You took change out but you didn't put the money in."

"Then you must not've seen what you thought you seen," Charlie said, "'cause I didn't take no money."

Charlie stared at Mickey, Kurtis Blow rapping about basketball in the background.

Mickey said, "Look, I wouldn't even say anything about it, but Harry said he was gonna fire you if he catches you stealing—"

"I wasn't stealing," Charlie said.

"Do whatever you want to do," Mickey said. "I'm just trying to help you out, but if you don't want my help, that's fine with me."

Mickey walked back to the stool and sat down and opened the newspaper. He was staring at the hockey scores without reading them.

Charlie shut off the music. For a while, Charlie remained behind the fish stands, then he came over to where Mickey was sitting.

"All right, I took it," Charlie said. "But it was just twenty bucks."

Mickey closed the newspaper.

"But the other day," Mickey said, "when I asked you—"

"I didn't want to get you involved. It's just something I'm doing myself, on my own."

"I could give a shit about the money," Mickey said, "but Harry was serious—he'll fire you."

"The fuck do I care?" Charlie said. "You think I need this shit-ass job? I can ring people's bells, ask 'em if I could rake the leaves off their lawn, and make more than I'm making here."

"So if you think you can make more money doing something else, then quit," Mickey said.

"Why is it any of your business what I do?" Charlie said.

"Because I don't want to see you get in trouble," Mickey said. "If Harry catches you he'll press charges."

"He won't catch me."

"What do you mean? He already found money missing one time. If he sees you—"

"Shit, I been takin' from that dumb-ass for two years," Charlie said, "and he ain't caught on yet."

"What're you talking about?" Mickey said. "He found money missing."

"All right, so I fucked up one time, but it won't happen again."

"How do you know?"

"Because I got it all figured out," Charlie said. "The money on the receipts adds up to the money on the register. Like the old man who was just here, right. Fish he bought cost twelve-fifty. I don't ring it up as a sale, I just open the drawer. I take the twenty, give him the seven-fifty change out of the register. Then, the end of the day or whenever, I go back to the register and put the seven-fifty back inside, so I get my twelve-fifty and the receipts add up. I usually take home an extra forty or fifty bucks a day."

"If you make a mistake again, he'll find out about it," Mickey said.

"But I won't make another mistake," Charlie said. "I'm gonna be careful from now on. I used to keep track of the numbers in my head—now I write them down on a piece of paper."

"You sure you want to do this?" Mickey said.

"I got no choice," Charlie said. "I got two brothers and my mother makes shit, answering phones for doctors, and Harry's money I can wipe my ass with. So I just do a little supplementing of my income—what's wrong with that? You think Harry and his rich-ass brother in Miami need that money? You don't think they got money to burn? I hear Harry on the phone with his stockbroker, talking about all these stocks he's buying—thousand shares of this, thousand shares of that—the guy's got money comin' out of his asshole. So what's the difference if I take some extra home with me or not?"

"If you need money why can't you get another job?" Mickey said. "Can't you work nights or weekends?"

Charlie was shaking his head.

"I got stuff to do at home, man. I gotta take my little brother to school in the morning, I gotta help him with his homework at night. I gotta keep an eye on him, make sure he don't join up with the wrong crowd. I got responsibilities."

A woman came into the store. Charlie took the order and Mickey watched as he made change from the register, then, when she left, he pocketed the ten-dollar bill she'd given him.

"Just be careful," Mickey said. "You better be keeping track of how much money you take out of the register."

"Twenty-two dollars and forty-five cents so far today," Charlie said.

"Still, you better watch out," Mickey said.

"I will, daddy, I will," Charlie said, smiling.

HEADING BACK TOWARD Albany Avenue, carrying a warm pizza box in front of him, Mickey spotted Filippo hanging out with his girlfriend Donna and a bunch of guys—Eddie Dugan, Rob Stefani, John Lyle—on the corner. They were all drinking beer out of paper bags, and Filippo had his arm around Donna's waist. Filippo looked over and saw Mickey. They stared at each other for a few seconds, then Filippo turned back toward the other guys and started talking again. As Mickey continued up the block, he looked back over his shoulder. Filippo was still talking to the other guys, but Donna was looking right at Mickey now with a blank expression. Mickey kept staring at Donna as he turned the corner.

Seeing Filippo hanging out with his friends, acting like he

would on any other night, angered the hell out of Mickey. Filippo should have been home mourning, and he definitely shouldn't have been out enjoying himself.

In his apartment, Mickey sat on the floor in his room, eating his meatball pizza. After a couple of slices he was full and he went into the kitchen and put the rest of the pie away in the fridge.

Mickey returned to his room and started watching *Dukes of Hazzard,* but he couldn't concentrate. He kept thinking about Rhonda, wondering what she was doing, if she was thinking about him right now too, if she missed him as much as he missed her. He imagined her with another guy, a Jewish guy, someone her father wanted her to be with.

He picked up the phone and dialed her number. When she answered he didn't know what to say.

"Uh . . . Rhonda?"

"Yes."

"It's Mickey."

She waited a few seconds then said, "Hi."

"I just called to see what's up," Mickey said.

"This isn't a good time," Rhonda said.

Mickey pictured the Jewish guy sitting next to her.

"I called you the other day," Mickey said. "Did you get my message?"

"Sorry, I've just been really busy."

"Yeah, I know, you had a big Thanksgiving dinner at your house."

"How did you know that?"

"I just figured you did."

"I really have to go now."

"Is somebody there?"

"No, I just have to go."

"Do you want to go to a movie with me tomorrow night?"

"I can't. I really have to go, okay?"

"Okay, but—"

She hung up. Mickey called her back and the answering machine picked up. When he called again a few seconds later the line was busy.

Mickey pictured Rhonda and her new boyfriend in Rhonda's room, on her bed, making out, starting to have sex. He tried calling her a few more times but the line was still busy, then he called Mrs. Turner.

"Oh my God, Mickey!"

Mrs. Turner sounded even more upset than she had the other day.

"What happened?" Mickey said, starting to panic himself. "What's going on?"

"Oh, God, Mickey," she said, crying. "Oh, God. It's not fair, it's not fair!"

"What?" Mickey said. "What happened?"

Mrs. Turner cried even harder and louder, breathing heavily. Finally, she said, "He's dead! They found his body in the Hudson this morning. My baby's dead!"

15

FOR A LONG time, Mrs. Turner couldn't speak clearly, but she finally explained what had happened. Early this morning, a guy fishing off a dock near Dobbs Ferry in Westchester had spotted a body floating in the Hudson. The body was badly decomposed but the police had determined that the person had been dead for about a week. The Westchester police contacted other police departments in the New York area about missing persons and found out about Chris. Using Chris's dental X rays the Westchester police were able to ID the body.

Mrs. Turner stopped talking and there were just the sounds of her sobbing. Mickey knew he had to say something, something that would sound right.

"I can't believe it," he said. "I just can't believe it."

"Why'd this have to happen to him?" Mrs. Turner said. "Why'd it have to happen to my little boy?"

"Do they know how he died?" Mickey said.

"He got shot," Mrs. Turner said. She cried for several seconds then said, "They found the bullet in his chest."

"Holy shit," Mickey said, trying to sound surprised. "Who could've shot him?"

"I got no idea," Mrs. Turner said. "Everybody loved Chris."

Mickey stayed on the phone with Mrs. Turner for a few more minutes, and he was relieved when she said she had to go.

Sitting at the end of his bed with his eyes closed, Mickey knew the police would come to talk to him soon. They would match Chris's blood to blood found in the Manhattan Beach house, and then they would talk to Chris's friends to see if they knew anything. Even if they denied it, the old guy who'd seen them getting into the car would be able to ID them. Mickey imagined Filippo breaking down and admitting everything, or, more likely, Filippo telling the cops Mickey Prada killed Chris.

Mickey couldn't believe Ralph had fucked up so badly, and he worried about the other things Ralph was supposed to get rid of—the laundry bags filled with their clothes and the things they had stolen. Mickey couldn't remember if he'd checked all the pockets of his pants. Maybe he'd left something in a pocket, or maybe Ralph or Filippo had.

At one point, Mickey dialed 911, ready to tell the police everything. He'd explain how Filippo had killed Chris by accident and how he'd had nothing to do with it. But when the operator answered, Mickey realized what he was doing and hung up. Calling the police now would be crazy. Even if they believed that Chris's death was accidental, they would still arrest Mickey for robbery—armed robbery. Mickey remembered being in the car Ralph had stolen on the way to Manhattan Beach that night. He'd had his chance to get out then and he didn't take it. All he could do now was pray he didn't get caught.

The rest of the evening Mickey waited for the police to arrive. Every time a car drove by he was convinced it was a police car, and every time a car stopped and a door closed he imagined it would only be seconds before his doorbell rang. He might have slept for an hour or two, but in the morning he felt like he'd been awake all night.

At work, every time a customer came in Mickey looked up from whatever he was doing, expecting to be arrested.

Charlie noticed Mickey acting strangely and said, "You all right?"

"Fine," Mickey said.

"You sure?" Charlie said, " 'cause you don't look too good."

"I said I'm fine," Mickey snapped.

"All right," Charlie said. "Damn."

Mickey went to lunch at John's Pizzeria, across the street from the fish store. After he ordered a slice and a grape soda, he turned around and saw a cop standing on line behind him.

Mickey felt his face getting hot but he tried to stay calm.

"How's it goin'?" the cop said to him.

"All right," Mickey said, his mouth so dry he could barely speak.

Mickey paid for his food and sat at a table in the back, facing the door. The cop took his time at the register, joking around with the guys behind the counter, then he took his order to go and got into his double-parked squad car.

As Mickey ate his slice quickly, taking big bites, he decided he had to stop living his life in fear. Maybe the police would catch him, maybe they wouldn't, but he just had to forget about it.

When Mickey returned to the fish store, Charlie was finishing ringing up a customer. Mickey watched Charlie keep the twenty the customer had given him and make change from the cash register. Maybe Charlie was right—if he was careful there was no way Harry would ever catch on. Mickey had seen Harry's books last year when Harry had asked for help getting his corporate tax return ready. The Vincent's Fish Market books were a mess, and there was no way for Harry to keep track of exactly how much money came into the store and how much went out.

When Charlie left on his lunch break, Mickey couldn't stop staring at the cash register. If he could make some fast money by stealing from Harry, he could pay off his debts to Artie and the funeral home and start college in the fall.

A few minutes later, a woman came into the store and bought twenty-eight dollars worth of fish. She handed Mickey two twenty-dollar bills. Mickey held the bills in his hand and gave her twelve dollars change from the register. When the woman left the store, Mickey pocketed the twenties.

The next customer came in and paid Mickey with a ten-dollar bill for an eight-dollar order. Mickey kept the ten and gave the customer two dollars from the register.

When Charlie returned from lunch, Mickey was in a better mood and said, "Hey, I just wanted to say sorry for the way I've been acting all day. I guess I was just upset about my friend Chris."

"What happened to him?" Charlie asked.

"He's dead," Mickey said.

"Seriously?" Charlie said.

"Yeah," Mickey said. "He was shot—last week, but they just found his body."

"Oh, shit," Charlie said. "Man, I'm sorry."

During the afternoon, Mickey took another sixty dollars from the register and then he replaced the change he had taken out. For the day he'd netted fifty-nine dollars.

When Harry came to the store at six o'clock, he looked at the day's receipts and said, "Slow day, huh?"

"Yeah," Mickey said, trying not to smile.

MICKEY WAS ON his way up the driveway, heading toward the entrance to his apartment, when a man's voice behind him said, "You Mickey Prada?"

Mickey turned around and saw two men in suits—a short, stocky guy with slicked-back blond hair and an older, taller guy with gray hair.

"Yeah," Mickey said thinking, This is it.

The taller man, the one who'd called out Mickey's name, said, "I'm Detective Frank Harris and this is my partner Matt Donnelly. We're with the Sixty-first Precinct, Manhattan Beach. We understand you were friends with Chris Turner."

"That's right," Mickey said, managing to stay calm.

"Mrs. Turner told us we could find you here," Harris explained. "Did Chris tell you where he was going last Saturday night?"

"Last Saturday night?" Mickey said, as if trying to remember.

"We believe he was shot to death during a robbery of a house on Hastings Street in Manhattan Beach last Saturday night," Harris said.

"A robbery?" Mickey said. "Jesus."

"Did he tell you anything about this?" Harris asked, opening a small pad.

"No way," Mickey said. "I had no idea."

"Were you friends with Chris a long time?" Harris asked.

"My whole life," Mickey said.

"Do you know a guy named Ralph DeMarco?"

"I don't know his last name," Mickey said, "but Chris has a friend Ralph on our bowling team."

"Heavy guy, balding?"

"Sounds like the same guy," Mickey said.

"Did Chris say anything to you," Donnelly said, "about doing anything with DeMarco last Saturday night?"

Mickey shook his head.

"When was the last time you saw Chris?" Harris asked.

"Last Thursday night," Mickey said. "I was over at his house watching TV."

"Just for the record," Harris said, "where were you last Saturday night?"

"Home," Mickey said, "watching TV in my room."

"Was anybody with you?"

"My father," Mickey said, "but he's dead now."

"Mrs. Turner told us," Harris said, "we're sorry for your loss."

The way Harris said it Mickey knew he couldn't give a shit.

"Thanks," Mickey said.

"Well, I think that should about do it for now," Harris said. He put his pad away in an inner-jacket pocket and took out a business card and handed it to Mickey. "Do us a favor. If you hear anything, anything you think we should know about, give me a call at that number. There's an answering machine so you can leave a message."

"So you really think he was killed robbing a house?" Mickey said.

"In all probability that's what happened," Harris said. "The bullet that we found in the victim's body matched a bullet found at the scene of the robbery. We think the bullets were fired from the same gun."

"Jesus," Mickey said.

Mickey watched the detectives walk away, then he went up to his apartment. He undressed and took a long shower. Eventually he fell asleep in front of the TV, but he kept waking up every hour. At six-thirty, just as the sun was starting to rise, he gave up trying to sleep and drove to the luncheonette on Nostrand and I. He sat at the counter and had bacon and eggs, orange juice, and a cup of black coffee. The guy next to Mickey got up and left a copy of the Sunday *Daily News* on the counter. Mickey thumbed through the main section, finding nothing about Chris, then he left the luncheonette and drove to Rhonda's block.

He parked directly across the street from her house. He checked his watch—seven-fifteen. It was too early to ring the bell; besides, her father might answer. He would just have to wait for her to come out. It was his day off work and he would wait all day if he had to.

At nine o'clock, Mickey was still sitting in his parked car, watching the house. No one had come or gone. Then, at around nine-thirty, the shades opened over the windows of the room on the second floor facing the street. Mickey wondered if this was Rhonda's room. His palms started to sweat as he imagined seeing her through the window. But whoever opened the shades moved away quickly, and Mickey couldn't tell who was there.

The stitches in Mickey's right hand were starting to itch badly, and he remembered how he had been supposed to go to a doctor to have them removed. Using the pen knife on his key chain Mickey started picking at the stitches, removing them one by one.

At about ten o'clock, Rhonda's father left the house. Mickey ducked down quickly, peering over the steering wheel as her father got into the station wagon that was parked in the driveway and drove away.

A few minutes later, Rhonda's stepmother left the house, wearing sweatpants and a sweatshirt, and Mickey ducked down again. He waited awhile then sat up, seeing she had jogged halfway up the block. He didn't hesitate. When she turned the corner, he got out of the car and walked quickly toward the house. He'd rehearsed what he was going to say, but now it was all jumbled in his head. It didn't matter. He wasn't going to blow this chance.

He rang the doorbell, counted to ten, and rang it again. He was about to ring it a third time when the door unlocked and opened. Rhonda was standing there in sweatpants and a big white T-shirt. Her hair was messy and she had no makeup on, not even lipstick. She looked like she had just woken up, but she still looked great.

"Hi," Mickey said, smiling.

Rhonda seemed surprised when she'd opened the door; now she just looked angry.

"What are you doing here?" she asked coldly.

"I just came to talk and tell you how sorry I am for whatever I did."

"You shouldn't be here," Rhonda said.

"I want to talk to you," Mickey said. "Come on, let me in."

"Why are you doing this?" Rhonda said.

"Please," Mickey said. "Maybe we could go somewhere. I have my car—"

"No," Rhonda said. "Look, I don't know why you can't understand this, but I don't want to see you anymore. You have to go."

"But I don't understand what I did wrong," Mickey said.

"You didn't do anything wrong. It's just . . . You just have to leave, okay?"

"It's just what?" Mickey said.

"It's nothing." Rhonda turned around for a second, toward the inside of the house.

"You have a guy in there?"

"What? . . . No."

"You're lying."

"Why would I lie?"

"Then why can't I come in?"

"You have to go home, Mickey. Please."

Rhonda tried to close the door, but Mickey stuck his foot in front.

"What's his name?" Mickey asked.

"Please get out of the way," Rhonda said.

Using his shoulder, Mickey pushed the door open and made it into the foyer.

"What's wrong with you?!" Rhonda screamed. "Get out of my house!"

Mickey looked beyond Rhonda but he didn't see anyone in the living room.

"Is he upstairs?" Mickey asked.

"There's nobody here," Rhonda said.

"Then what's wrong with you?" Mickey said. "Why are you treating me this way?"

"You better get out of here right now," Rhonda said. "I'm warning you, I'll scream for help."

"I know you love me," Mickey said. "I remember how you looked at me that first time we met in the fish store. We're perfect together."

"Please just leave me alone," Rhonda said, backing away.

"I can't live without you," Mickey said.

"What are you talking about?" Rhonda said. "You don't even know me."

Mickey took a step toward her. She grabbed the object nearest her—a heavy glass vase from on top of a side table— and held it above her head.

"Leave right now, you lunatic," she said, the vase shaking in her hands.

"Come on," Mickey said, "just put that down so we can talk."

Mickey lunged toward her and tried to grab the vase.

"Come on, give it to me."

"Let go!"

"Come on."

Mickey was starting to pry the vase loose when it smashed onto the floor, shattering glass everywhere.

"I'm sorry," Mickey said, "I didn't mean to do that. Please stop crying. Just stop crying!"

Mickey tried to hug Rhonda when the front door opened behind him. Mickey turned and saw Rhonda's father enter the house, holding the Sunday *Times*.

"What the hell's going on here?" her father asked.

Rhonda rushed to her father and stood next to him.

"What the hell are you doing here?" her father said to Mickey.

"He just came in," Rhonda said, crying. "He wouldn't leave. He wouldn't leave!"

"That's not true," Mickey said, "I just—"

Rhonda's father grabbed Mickey's arm near the shoulder and pulled him toward the door. Her father wasn't a big man—he was several inches shorter than Mickey and probably about ten pounds lighter. Mickey stopped, a few feet in front of the door, and her father couldn't pull him any farther.

"Get out of here, you son of a bitch, or I'll call the police," her father said.

"This is just a misunderstanding," Mickey said. "I was just trying to talk to her when the vase broke—"

"I don't give a shit what happened, I want you out of my house right now!"

He yanked on Mickey's arm again. Mickey wouldn't budge and her father was pulling the sleeve of his shirt, stretching the collar, twisting Mickey awkwardly. Mickey pushed him back, trying to get free, and then her father pushed his open hand into Mickey's neck. Mickey had a sudden gagging sensation then he cocked his fist.

"Don't!" Rhonda shouted.

Mickey lowered his fist, realizing what he had almost done.

"I didn't mean that," Mickey said to Rhonda. "I just wanted to talk to you."

Rhonda was crying again. Mickey knew it was too late. Whatever he said now would come out all wrong.

Rhonda's father said, "Just get the hell out of here right now before I call the police!"

Mickey looked at Rhonda. She ran into another room. Mickey turned and walked slowly out of the house as the door slammed behind him.

16

THE NEXT MORNING at work, Mickey called Rhonda every fifteen minutes or so, but the line was constantly busy. Finally, at around one o'clock, he reached the answering machine.

"Rhonda, I hope you're listening to this message. Rhonda, it's Mickey. Look, I'm sorry, okay? I wish you could understand how sorry I am. Please, try to understand. It was just because of my father, I think. It's just been really rough on me, you know, and now I found out my best friend is dead too. He was shot and . . . Look, I know that's no excuse for doing what I did, but I'm just asking you to call me, just to talk, okay? You're all I have right now and I can't lose you too. And if Rhonda's father or stepmother are listening to this, I want you to both know that I'm sorry from the bottom of my heart. Please call me, Rhonda, okay? Please."

The rest of the day, Mickey continued to take breaks, calling his answering machine to see if Rhonda had returned his call. She hadn't. After work, he went to meet Artie at the bookie joint to make a payment on his debt. He

turned onto Kings Highway and saw Angelo Santoro walking along the sidewalk toward East Twenty-seventh Street.
Angelo looked nothing like he usually did. He was wearing
jeans and a navy blue hooded sweatshirt, his face all scruffy.
Mickey tried to pull over but a van was riding his tail and he
had to make a right onto Bedford Avenue. He went around
the block and turned back onto Kings Highway on Twenty-
fourth Street. He drove slowly, looking around in every
direction, but Angelo was gone.

"SORRY I COULDN'T make your old man's wake, how was it?"
Artie said.

Mickey was sitting next to Artie at a bridge table in the
corner of the bookie joint. There were about twenty other
people crammed into the room, sitting at the other tables or
walking around. *Racing Forms*, betting slips, and partially
eaten doughnuts and bagels were spread around the tables.

"Only a few people showed," Mickey said.

"Shit," Artie said, looking up from a *Lawton*, the tip sheet
he was reading. "If I'da known I—"

"It's all right," Mickey said. "It's his fault anyway. I mean
my father wasn't exactly the most likable guy in the world."

"I know what you mean," Artie said. "I remember I'd try
to talk to him at the track sometimes, say, 'Who do you like
in this race?' or something like that and he'd say, 'Why, you
writing a book?' I'm not saying that's such a bad thing, but if
a guy asks you who you like you can tell him, I mean even if
you're gonna go off and bet a different horse. It's just called
being polite, you know what I mean?"

"My father sure as hell wasn't polite," Mickey said.

"You got that right," Artie said. "So you cremated him, huh?"

"Yeah," Mickey said.

"What did you do with the ashes?"

"Dumped 'em at Aqueduct."

"No shit?" Artie said, smiling. "Maybe I'll do that, I mean put it in my will. That wouldn't be so bad, being at the racetrack forever. Beats the hell out of rotting in some cemetery in butt fuck. But I wouldn't wanna be at Aqueduct. I'd like to be at some classy racetrack, you know? Maybe Saratoga or one of those French tracks. You know, with all that nice green grass."

Mickey coughed. "I better get out of here," he said, "before I catch cancer."

Mickey took an envelope out of his pocket and handed it to Artie. Inside the envelope were two hundred dollars in twenties and tens. Mickey had taken some money from the register at work earlier in the day; the rest had come out of his paycheck.

Artie, looking at *Lawton* again, took the envelope from Mickey quickly and put it right in his pocket without opening it. The bookie joint wasn't Artie's turf and he didn't want anyone to see him collecting money here.

"Look at this," Artie said, "*Lawton* had four fuckin' winners today, one of them was a ninety-dollar horse. But you know if you bought this sheet this morning and played all the picks, you wouldn'ta had one winner. When was the last time you heard somebody say, 'I swept the card today, it was a good thing I used *Lawton*?'"

Artie ripped up the *Lawton* sheet and tossed the pieces onto the table in front of him.

Mickey said, "I remember what I wanted to ask you. It's about Angelo Santoro . . ."

"The mobster who can't pick a winner at football," Artie said.

"I know he can't pick a winner but I don't know about the first part."

"What do you mean?" Artie said. "I thought you said you found out he was legit."

"He paid me the money," Mickey lied, "but I still don't know if he's in the mob. I remember you said you could ask around, maybe somebody heard of him."

"What do you care if he's in the mob or not?" Artie said. "I mean let's say it *was* all a scam. What difference is that gonna make to you? You got suckered any way you look at it."

"Whatever," Mickey said. "I just thought if you knew somebody and you could find something out I'd be curious to know. It's no big deal."

"All right, I'll ask around," Artie said. "See what I can come up with."

"Thanks," Mickey said. He got up to leave.

"Hey, who you like tonight?" Artie asked.

"Like?" Mickey said.

"Jets or Dolphins?"

"I don't like anybody," Mickey said.

"Smart man," Artie said. "Smart man."

WHEN MICKEY CAME home there was one message on his answering machine. Mickey closed his eyes as he pressed PLAY, hoping to hear Rhonda's voice, but the message was from Mrs. Turner. Last night, Mrs. Turner had called to let Mickey know that Chris's funeral would be held on Wednesday morning, and Mickey couldn't understand why she had called again tonight.

After pacing his apartment awhile, Mickey returned the call.

"Hi, it's Mickey."

"Mickey," Mrs. Turner said, sounding strange. Mickey couldn't tell if his call had woken her up or if she'd been drinking.

"You left a message for me," Mickey said.

"I did?" she said. "Oh, yeah, I did. It's about Chris—you know you were his best friend, don't you? Chris loved you, he really really loved you, Mickey, and I think you should say somethin' at the funeral."

"I don't know if that's such a good idea," Mickey said.

"Why not?" she said, suddenly talking louder, almost yelling. Now Mickey was sure she was drunk. "One of Chris's friends's gotta say somethin' and I don't know who else to ask. I never liked Filippo and I don't know his other friends too well. You gotta do it, Mickey."

"All right," Mickey said. "I mean if you want me to."

Mickey wanted to hang up but Mrs. Turner said, "You heard that crap they're saying, didn't you?"

"Crap?" Mickey said.

"That Chris was robbin' a house," Mrs. Turner said.

"Oh yeah," Mickey said. "That's what the detectives told me."

"I don't believe it for a second," Mrs. Turner said. "I know Chris had problems, but he wouldn't rob a house. Not my Chrissy."

"I'm sure the police'll find out what happened eventually," Mickey said.

"They better," Mrs. Turner said. "If I just knew what happened it'd make it so much easier. It's all the not knowing that's killin' me."

MICKEY AND CHARLIE were laying out the fresh fish on the ice when Francesca, an old Puerto Rican woman, came into the store. Francesca was a regular at Vincent's, coming in every Tuesday to buy a week's worth of fish for her family.

"I got this one," Mickey said to Charlie. Then he said, "How ya doin', Francesca? What can I get for you today?"

"What's fresh?" the old woman asked.

"Fluke's good," Mickey said. "We also got some really nice striped bass. Twenty-pounders."

Francesca ordered a pound of fluke, a pound of striped bass, a pound of porgies, and a half each of shrimp, mussels, and clams. As Mickey filled the order Francesca told him about how her grandson Steven had just been accepted to college at Brown. The order came to a little over forty-two dollars.

"Let's call it forty-two even," Mickey said.

Francesca gave Mickey exact change. Mickey saw that Charlie was busy, laying out fish, and Mickey opened the register and closed it, keeping the money in his hand.

"Have a great day," Mickey said.

During the rest of the day, Mickey stole another sixty-four dollars. At six-thirty, Harry returned to the store and checked the day's receipts. Mickey was cleaning up the front of the store, getting ready to close, and Charlie was cleaning in the back.

"Another slow day, huh?" Harry said.

"Yeah," Mickey said, continuing mopping, not looking up.

"I wonder why that is," Harry said. "I mean the weather's been good."

"Probably just one of those things," Mickey said.

On the way home, Mickey stopped at the supermarket and bought groceries with some of the money he'd stolen. Walking up Avenue K, carrying the paper shopping bags, Mickey spotted a car from a driving school, with a triangle-shaped advertisement on its roof; it reminded him of how Rhonda had said that she wanted him to teach her how to drive sometime.

When Mickey got home his appetite was gone, so he went into his father's room and continued cleaning out the closet and drawers. He took the filled garbage bags out to the curb, making several trips.

At around seven-thirty, Mickey called Artie.

"Gotta hang up on you," Artie said. "People are trying to call for the Knicks."

"I just wanted to see if you found out anything about Angelo Santoro," Mickey said.

"Oh yeah," Artie said. "I talked to a guy I know's connected. Like I thought, he said there's no Angelo Santoro in the Colombo family. The only Santoro he's heard of is Salvadore Santoro in the Lucchese family."

"Is he sure?" Mickey said.

"I'm just telling you what he told me," Artie said. "Maybe Angelo's in another family—Gambino, Bonanno. Or maybe I was right and he was putting one over on you. Lemme go, people're trying to get through."

Mickey slammed down the phone. Later, he started working on a speech for Chris's funeral. He kept writing sentences, crossing them out, and starting over again. Finally, he tore the paper into pieces, deciding he would just have to wing it.

17

WEARING THE SAME outfit he'd worn to his father's wake, Mickey arrived at the Guarino Funeral Home on Flatlands Avenue. A woman at the door directed Mickey to a room in the back where people for the Chris Turner funeral were gathering.

There seemed to be at least fifty people standing around, talking. Mickey saw Chris's mother, crying as some other woman was consoling her; then Mickey spotted Chris's father, on the other side of the room. Mickey hadn't seen Mr. Turner in years and he was a little surprised to see him at the funeral. Mickey didn't think Mrs. Turner had stayed in touch with him.

Mr. Turner made eye contact with Mickey, and Mickey went over to say hi.

"Mickey, hey, look at you," Mr. Turner said, putting his arm around Mickey's back. "You're what, a foot taller than me now?"

Mr. Turner had lost more of his hair and the rest of it had turned gray; otherwise, he hadn't changed much. He was about Chris's height and he looked a lot like Chris, especially around the mouth and eyes.

"I'm really sorry," Mickey said.

"Thanks, Mick, I appreciate that. I just wish I was around more these past few years. I wish I knew him better, you know?"

Mickey wanted to say, If you wanted to know him better maybe you shouldn't've run off and left him with an alcoholic to raise him. Instead he said, "I know Chris didn't have any hard feelings about it."

"You mean that?" Mr. Turner said.

"Yeah, he talked about you all the time," Mickey lied. "He was always talking about all the good times he had with you when he was growing up."

"Yeah, we did have a lot of good times, didn't we?" Mr. Turner said, managing a smile.

As Mickey and Mr. Turner talked about their memories of Chris, Mickey noticed Ralph, Filippo, and Donna, standing near the entrance to the room. Donna noticed Mickey first then Ralph looked in Mickey's direction. Ralph and Mickey stared at each other for maybe a second, then Ralph turned away and Mickey shifted his attention back toward Mr. Turner.

Mickey was hardly paying attention as Mr. Turner went on about the times he drove Chris and Mickey to Little League baseball games and to play in the video arcade at Kings Plaza. Finally someone came over to pay their respects to Mr. Turner, and Mickey was able to slip away.

Mickey went over to Mrs. Turner—smelling alcohol on her breath as he kissed her—and told her how sorry he was.

Then he left the room and went down the hallway to use the bathroom.

On the way out of the bathroom, a girl's voice said, "Hey, Mickey."

Mickey looked over and saw Donna standing off to the side. Mickey had never spoken to Donna before and he was surprised she knew his name.

"Come here a second," she said, waving Mickey into a room off the hallway.

Mickey looked around and didn't see Filippo, Ralph, or anyone else who might be watching, and then he followed Donna.

It was hard to believe Donna was only sixteen. She looked thirty, in a tight low-cut black dress with her cleavage pushing out. Her hair was big and frizzy, spreading out in every direction, and she reeked of perfume. She was wearing so much makeup it was hard to tell what her face looked like underneath.

Mickey remembered how good Rhonda always looked, wearing hardly any makeup.

"I gotta ask you somethin' about Chris," Donna said.

"What?" Mickey asked. He really didn't feel like talking to her or anyone.

"Do you know what happened to him?" she asked.

Mickey hesitated, wondering if Filippo had told her anything about the robbery. He was dumb enough to do something like that.

"No," Mickey said. "All I know is he was shot in some house in Manhattan Beach."

"The police talked to you?" Donna asked.

"Yeah," Mickey said. "I mean just to ask me if I knew any-thing, but I said I didn't. Why?"

"Just curious," Donna said. "You were friends with Chris, right? I mean like *good* friends."

"Yeah," Mickey said.

"Did you see him that night?"

"No," Mickey said. "I was home watching TV."

"Filippo said he was by Ralph's watchin' pornos. I don't know if I believe him or not. I mean I believe he watches pornos, but I don't know if I believe he was watchin' pornos that night."

"Why not?" Mickey asked. "I mean, why would he lie to you?"

"I don't know," Donna said. "It's just . . . I just wanted to see if you knew something, something Filippo didn't tell me, but I guess you don't know nothin' else, huh?"

"Sorry," Mickey said.

"Thanks, anyway," Donna said, then she smiled at Mickey, looking at him up and down. "You look pretty good all dressed up, you know?"

"Thanks," Mickey said.

"I don't know what's goin' on with me and Filippo," she said, "but maybe you wanna come over to my house some-time just to, you know, hang out."

Donna gave Mickey another sexy smile.

"Maybe," Mickey said, thinking about Rhonda again.

"You better go out before me," Donna said. "Filippo'll get mad if he knows I was talkin' to you."

Mickey left the room and saw that people had started to file into the chapel, where the service was going to be held.

Mickey took a seat in the second row, by the aisle, so he could get up easily when he was called to make his speech.

First the funeral director spoke. Although the old, pale, gray-haired guy knew a lot of details about Chris's life—when he was born, what schools he went to, his parents' names—it was obvious he didn't really *know* Chris, and he kept looking down at an index card while he was talking, squinting to see the words on it.

When the funeral director finished, Chris's cousin Joey went up to the podium and told stories about some of the good times he and Chris had growing up. The stories made people cry. Mickey was crying too, thinking about what Mrs. Turner had told him, how "the not knowing" was killing her. For years, after Mickey's mother was killed in the hit and run, Mickey had wondered who the driver was. Sometimes, when Mickey was riding in the backseat of his father's car, he'd look at the drivers of other cars they passed and wonder if he or she were the one.

Mickey's turn came to speak and his mouth was suddenly dry. Except for a few times in school, he had never spoken to a group of people before, and he felt like everyone who was staring at him knew the truth, that he had been with Chris the night Chris was killed and that he'd lied to the police. Mickey started talking, but he didn't know what he was saying. He knew he meant to talk about how Chris was his best friend and could always make him laugh and how much he was going to miss him, but all his words and sentences came out jumbled and he wasn't sure he was making any sense. A few times, he couldn't hear himself talk and the faces of the people in the audience seemed to turn white.

Mickey ended his speech by saying something about how much Chris loved his parents. Then he said, "Thank you," and left the podium, feeling dazed and unsteady on his feet. As he sat down, he was surprised to notice several people in the front rows crying, blowing their noses into tissues. Mrs. Turner, sitting in front of Mickey, turned around and squeezed Mickey's hand and whispered, "Thank you." Then Mickey looked to his left, and Mr. Turner winked at him and smiled. Mickey decided he probably hadn't done as badly as he'd thought.

The funeral ended and people filed out of the chapel, the front rows emptying first. As Mickey passed Ralph and Filippo he glanced in their direction, but they were looking away. Donna looked at Mickey, though, and smiled. Her eyes were bloodshot and her mascara was running from crying.

It was after eleven-thirty. Mickey had to be at work by noon, which was fine with him. He definitely wasn't in the mood to go to a cemetery.

18

MICKEY STOPPED HOME to drop off his car and to change into jeans and a sweatshirt. Walking to work, turning off Avenue J onto Flatbush, he saw Angelo Santoro.

Today Angelo was wearing his usual dark suit, walking past Vincent's Fish Market, about fifty yards ahead of Mickey. Mickey walked faster, trying to catch up.

Angelo turned the corner onto Avenue K. Mickey started jogging, then running, and turned the corner himself.

"Angelo!" Mickey called out, suddenly out of breath, even though he'd only run a short distance.

The man ahead of him turned around, and Mickey realized he'd made a mistake. From behind, the guy had looked like Angelo with his stocky shoulders and black suit, but this guy had a full graying beard and looked about sixty years old.

"Sorry," Mickey said, "I thought you were somebody else."

Mickey walked slowly back toward the fish store, then he stopped, trying to pull himself together. When he entered the store Charlie was busy with a customer.

"What's up?" Charlie said.

Without even looking at Charlie, Mickey went through the swinging doors to the back. He put on his apron and washed his hands then returned to the front. The customer was gone.

"How was the funeral?" Charlie asked.

"Like any funeral, I guess," Mickey said.

"You don't look too good," Charlie said. "Your eyes look like you got beat up. You should think about takin' a vacation. Seriously, man. You've been goin' through some rough shit lately. You should take your woman and go away someplace romantic."

Suddenly angry, Mickey said, "Yeah, that sounds like a great idea."

"Damn, I was just making a suggestion," Charlie said. "I just thought you should get away someplace, to an island or something. You ever been to Jamaica?"

Mickey shook his head.

"You gotta go to Jamaica, man," Charlie said. "My father was Jamaican, so I still got all my relatives there. I used to go in high school, but I haven't been in like five years. Man, I wanna go back so bad. They got these beaches on the north side of the island. Sunsets, palm trees, the drinks with them little umbrellas inside—just like the postcards."

Mickey looked away toward the door, where a customer was entering the store. Mickey took the woman's order then got a large container from behind the counter and said, "Sorry, did you say shrimp or scallops?"

"Scallops," the woman said.

Mickey scooped a pound of scallops into the container then filled the rest of the woman's order. The total came to twenty-six dollars and change. At the register, Mickey looked to his right at Charlie. Charlie was only a few feet away, but he was busy, cutting fillets. Mickey opened the register and gave the woman change for thirty dollars, but kept the twenty and the ten in his hand as he shut the register. As the woman left, Mickey slid the bills into his pocket.

"Another place you should go is Cancún," Charlie went on to Mickey. "I went there with my cousin for a week when I was eighteen. We went for spring break. That was crazy. Drinking, dancing. The girls down in Cancún, they know how to dance. They dance all night, never stop. I think I slept two hours the whole time. You been to Miami?"

Mickey was behind Charlie, rinsing knives in the sink.

"Nah," Mickey said.

"You know you can take a cruise from Miami to the Caribbean," Charlie said. "That's what I'd like to do—go on one of them cruises. You can party all the time, all night and day. I'd like to go to a lot of places. All the Caribbean islands, Puerto Rico, Europe, South America. What about you?"

"What about me?" Mickey said.

"Where're some of the places you been to?"

"I haven't been anywhere," Mickey said.

"What do you mean?" Charlie said. "You must go on vacation sometime, right?"

"No, not really," Mickey said.

"Not even when you was a kid?"

Mickey shook his head.

"You kiddin' me? You never been anywhere? Not one time?"

Mickey shook his head again.

"You never been on an airplane?"

"No," Mickey said.

"*How* old are you?" Charlie said.

The bell above the door rang and Harry entered the store. Harry pointed at Mickey and said, "All right, asshole, get the fuck over here."

"Why? What's going on?" Mickey asked.

"I said get your ugly fuckin' ass over here," Harry said.

Mickey came around the counter and stopped a few feet in front of Harry.

"What's goin' on?" Charlie said.

"Just get back to work," Harry said. Then he said to Mickey, "All right, lemme see what you got in your pockets."

"My pockets?" Mickey said, trying to come up with a way out of this but knowing there was none.

"You got a marked ten and a marked twenty in one of your pockets," Harry said. "Just gimme my fuckin' money, you little piece of shit!"

Mickey hesitated. He looked over at Charlie and saw Charlie's confused expression. With his eyes Mickey tried to tell Charlie, Just keep your mouth shut.

"Come on, let's go, I know you have it," Harry said. "That was my cousin Barbara in here before. She saw you open the register and take my fuckin' money. Show it to me!"

Slowly, Mickey reached into his right front pocket, removed the two bills, and held them out for Harry to take.

Harry snatched the money from Mickey and said, "You little fuckin' son of a bitch, I should kick the shit outta you right here. You think I'm stupid, huh? That it? You think I'm fuckin' stupid? Tellin' me business is slow, you son of a bitch."

"I'm sorry," Mickey said.

"Fuck you," Harry said, his eyes bulging. "You think I care if you're fuckin' sorry? I'd like to send you through the fuckin' wall, what I'd like to do."

"Yo, Harry, man, I think you're making a mistake," Charlie said.

"There's no mistake," Mickey said, rushing to cut Charlie off. "I took the money, I admit it, but I'll give it all back."

"Damn right you will," Harry said. "You're gonna give me back every fuckin' cent you stole from me, *plus* interest, you fuckin' thief. But no way you're gonna get off that easy. I already called the cops on you. They're on their way over here right now. I'm pressin' charges against you. You're scared, huh? That's right, be scared. I don't give a shit if you're scared, you fuckin' scumbag. How long's this been goin' on? Since you started working here? You been stealing from me for three fuckin' years?"

"No," Mickey said.

"No, what? What the fuck does 'no' mean?"

"No, I just started stealing . . . recently," Mickey said, staring at Charlie who still looked confused.

"Why should I believe anything you tell me, you little piece of shit?" Harry said. "You've been lying to me for . . . for how long?" Harry turned to Charlie. "You know I thought it was you at first. Sorry, but that's what I thought. So I asked Pinocchio here if he thought you'd steal and he says, 'No, Charlie would never steal.' Meanwhile, it's this little fuck who's the thief. How stupid am I, huh? How fuckin' stupid?"

A few minutes later, two police officers entered the store. Harry explained to them that he'd caught Mickey stealing and that Mickey might have stolen hundreds or thousands of dollars over the past few years. The older officer asked Mickey if what Harry said was true and Mickey said he'd only taken a few hundred dollars. The officer placed Mickey under arrest and the other officer handcuffed him. As Mickey was being led out of the store, he looked over at Charlie and Mickey blinked once slowly, trying to say, Don't worry about it.

Passersby stopped and watched as the officers led Mickey to a police car parked up the block. They took him to the police precinct on Lawrence Avenue, where he had to wait in a holding cell for about two hours before he was fingerprinted and photographed. They made him wait in the cell for another two hours, then he was taken downtown to Central Booking, where a guard led him through a maze of large cells the guard called the tombs. The cells had no windows and were lit by fluorescent lights. There were dozens of prisoners in each cell, packed tightly, and it was very noisy, with all the prisoners talking and yelling. The dank air smelled like piss.

Mickey was put into a cell with about thirty other guys who all looked like hardened criminals. Mickey knew he should probably be afraid, but he didn't care about anything. He sat Indian-style in the corner of the cell with his eyes closed, hoping the whole world would disappear.

A group of six black guys at the other end of the cell were laughing loudly; Mickey opened his eyes and saw they were looking in his direction. Mickey could only make out an occasional word—"white boy," "bitch," "faggot." He looked away, trying to ignore them, but when he looked over again the guys were coming toward him. One tall guy with a close-cut Afro and a gold tooth was walking ahead of the others. The tall guy stopped a few feet in front of Mickey and said, "What'd you do, white boy?"

Mickey looked away again, when the tall guy kicked him hard in the shin. Mickey keeled over, grabbing his leg. The guys were laughing harder.

"I said what'd you do, white boy? You rape somebody? Put your little white dick up somebody's ass?"

The guys laughed again.

"Look at me, white boy," the tall guy said. "Yo, I said look at me."

Mickey, his shin still stinging, looked up. The tall guy spit in Mickey's face. The guys laughed harder as Mickey wiped his cheek and forehead.

"I know what you did," the tall guy said. "White boy took the money from the bank. That's why he here. White boy took the money from the bank."

The tall guy started poking Mickey with his index fingers, saying, "White boy took the money from the bank." The other guys joined in saying, "White boy took the money from the bank," as Mickey held his head down and closed his eyes.

The tall guy kneeled down in front of Mickey and started slapping him in the face, softly at first, then harder, and Mickey's face started stinging. Mickey tried to push the tall guy away, but the other guys lifted Mickey up by the arms and held him as the tall guy continued slapping Mickey saying, "White boy took the money from the bank. White boy took the money from the bank. White boy took the money from the bank. . . ."

Finally, two guards came into the cell and pulled the guys away. Mickey's lower lip was bleeding and his face felt bruised. The cops took Mickey down the hallway to another crowded cell. Mickey sat in the corner, staring blankly. About an hour later, one of the cops brought him some wet paper towels for his face.

A man came around with dinner for the prisoners— salami sandwiches. A few hours later, around midnight, a bored-looking guy in a wrinkled suit who said he was with the Criminal Justice Agency came to talk to Mickey. The man asked Mickey questions about his case and Mickey answered them. Mickey said he wanted to plead guilty.

Mickey had to wait until the next day before a judge was able to see him. He tried to sleep, lying on the floor, but it was impossible under the bright lights, with all the noise, and with his face still throbbing.

At around two the next afternoon, Mickey was brought to the courtroom. He was assigned to a lawyer who told the judge Mickey was pleading guilty to the charge of grand larceny. Since this was his first offense, the judge, a woman who reminded Mickey of Mrs. Litsky, his third-grade teacher who'd always hated him, agreed to let Mickey go without bail. A hearing date was scheduled for late December, and the judge ordered Mickey to stay away from the fish store and from Harry Giordano.

It was after four-thirty in the afternoon when Mickey was finally released from Central Booking. Beat up, exhausted, and squinting against the bright setting sun, he stepped out onto Schermerhorn Street. It was much colder and windier than it had been yesterday, and Mickey was freezing in a sweatshirt and no jacket.

He walked over to Flatbush Avenue and took the bus home. He fell asleep with his head sagging to one side, and when he woke up he realized that he was on Avenue T, about six stops past where he'd meant to get off. Mickey took a bus back in the opposite direction and by the time he got home it was almost six o'clock and pitch-dark.

Mickey went right to his bed and collapsed. It seemed like just a few seconds later the doorbell was ringing. Mickey ignored the sounds, figuring it was happening in a dream, but the bell kept ringing and he gradually realized he wasn't asleep.

Still wearing the clothes he had been wearing for the past two days, with a sudden splitting headache, Mickey went downstairs. Blackie was barking like crazy and someone had their finger on the doorbell. Mickey opened the door and saw the two detectives, Harris and Donnelly, who had questioned Mickey about Chris's death.

"We didn't wake you, did we?" Harris asked. "It's only nine-thirty—we didn't think you'd be asleep yet. Then again, we understand you had a rough night."

"Lemme guess," Donnelly said, "you got that fat lip in the pen down at Central Booking. You're lucky that's all you got. A kid like you, deer-in-the-headlights-kinda look, might wind up in the ICU on life support."

Blackie's barking was making Mickey's headache even worse.

"So what's going on?" Mickey asked.

"What's going on is we need to ask you some questions," Harris said. "We can either do it here or at the precinct. Your choice."

Wondering how his life could possibly get any worse, Mickey said, "Come in."

The detectives followed Mickey upstairs and into the kitchen. There were two chairs at the table. Detective Donnelly and Mickey sat while Detective Harris remained standing.

"So a funny thing happened this afternoon," Harris said. "I was just checking up on some people I'd talked to about Chris Turner's murder, and what do I find but a rap sheet on you. Your first arrest, just yesterday afternoon. Talk about timing, huh?"

"That has nothing to do with Chris," Mickey said.

"Nothing, huh?" Harris said. He looked at Donnelly. "Funny, I don't think it has nothing to do with it, how about you Matt?"

Donnelly shook his head.

"See," Harris went on, "when a guy I questioned about a robbery pleads guilty to another robbery I can't help thinking there's a connection. You were with Chris Turner that night, weren't you?"

"No," Mickey said.

"Come on," Harris said, "might as well admit it. You and Chris were there and who else was with you? Was Ralph DeMarco there?"

"No," Mickey said.

"No, DeMarco wasn't there, but you were there—"

"No, I wasn't there and I have no idea if Ralph was there," Mickey said.

Harris smiled and looked over at Donnelly.

"So why'd you rip off your boss?" Donnelly asked. "You short on cash?"

"I made a mistake," Mickey said.

"I didn't ask if you made a mistake," Donnelly said. "I asked why you did it."

Mickey looked away, thinking, then he said, "I needed the money."

"So you stole because you needed money," Donnelly said. "How original. What was the problem, you didn't make enough robbing that house with your friends?"

"I didn't rob any house," Mickey said.

Donnelly turned to Harris.

Harris said to Mickey, "Look, we know you were at the house, so maybe if you tell us who was with you and how Chris Turner got shot, then maybe we'll take it a little easy on you. I mean this could be your second arrest in two days. I hope you realize how serious this could be for you."

"You want me to lie and tell you I robbed a house with Chris?" Mickey said. "Is that what you want me to do?"

"No, we want you to tell us the truth," Harris said.

"I'm telling you the fucking truth," Mickey said. "I wasn't there. I was home that night watching the Knicks."

"And isn't it a coincidence," Harris said, "the only person who can vouch for your story happens to be dead."

"I don't care if you believe me or not," Mickey said.

"All right, we're gonna be honest with you ourselves now,"

Donnelly said. "No more bullshit, all right? We don't think you had anything to do with your friend's murder. We think you just got caught up, wrong place at the wrong time. So why make things any more difficult for you? Why not fess up? Tell us who was there with you, what happened, and we'll let you off easy."

"I wasn't there," Mickey said. "How many times do you need to hear me say it? I wasn't there."

Harris approached Mickey suddenly. With his face an inch or two in front of Mickey's, he said, "Look, prick, you're lucky as hell we didn't run you in already. We could've done it, you know, and the judge wouldn't've let you off this time. It would've cost you fifty, maybe a hundred grand to see the light of day again. You don't have that kind of money, do you? No, I didn't think so. You had fifty grand lying around, you wouldn't be ripping off your boss and robbing a house."

"I didn't rob any house!" Mickey screamed.

"Bullshit!" Harris screamed back.

"I want a lawyer," Mickey said in a suddenly calm voice. "If you won't give me a lawyer you'll have to arrest me."

Harris, still leaning over the table, looked over at Donnelly.

"Look at this, Matt," Harris said. "Kid gets arrested one time he's an expert on the law, knows all his fuckin' rights."

Harris backed away and motioned to Donnelly with his head. Donnelly stood up.

"All right, you want us to leave, we'll leave," Harris said to Mickey. "But you might want to think about what we said. You're a young guy—twenty years or longer in the pen's gonna go by real slow."

The detectives left and Mickey remained at the kitchen table with his head in his hands. He was too exhausted to be worried about anything the detectives had said, and he knew they probably didn't have anything on him, anyway. They didn't even say anything about the old man on the street, so the guy must not have come forward.

Mickey was starting to doze and decided he should eat something. He wasn't hungry but he realized he hadn't eaten anything since a couple of rolls for breakfast in prison.

Mickey nibbled on leftovers from the fridge—mushy Chinese food, hardened pizza. His head was still throbbing and his shin hurt where the guy had kicked him last night. He looked in the bathroom medicine chest for some aspirin but couldn't find any. He went into his room and collapsed on the bed.

Bright rays of sunshine were coming through the window into his room. He looked at the clock near his bed and saw the time—12:14. He went to the bathroom then returned to bed and fell back asleep.

When he woke up again it was dark outside. The clock read 5:04. He fell asleep again and the ringing phone woke him up. Reaching for the receiver, he saw it was after midnight. He had missed an entire day.

"Mickey, it's Ralph."

Before Mickey could say anything, Ralph said, "Meet me in an hour, Midwood Field, by the handball courts."

"Why?" Mickey asked. "What's going on?"

"Just be there," Ralph said.

Mickey tried to say something else, but Ralph had already hung up.

19

MICKEY CLOSED HIS eyes and dozed again. A few minutes later, he woke up and forced himself to get out of bed.

Although he had slept for over twenty-four hours straight—thirty including the time before the detectives arrived—he was still exhausted. He put on jeans and a sweatshirt then went into the bathroom and splashed his face with cold water. It didn't help. His legs were weak and his knees felt like they were buckling.

Midwood Field was over a mile away from Mickey's house. Mickey and Chris used to go there sometimes after school and practice kicking field goals. Mickey remembered the time he was kicking and Chris pulled the ball away at the last moment, like Lucy always did to Charlie Brown, and Mickey slipped on the frozen turf and fell flat on his ass.

Mickey parked on Avenue K, near East Seventeenth Street, across the street from the handball courts next to the football field. There was a group of about ten teenagers, some wearing Midwood High School jackets, drinking beer out of paper bags and listening to music on a car stereo. It felt like it was the coldest night of the fall so far. Sitting in his parked car, wearing just a windbreaker over his sweat-shirt, Mickey was shivering and he wished he'd worn a warmer jacket.

Mickey waited in the car for about five minutes, then he decided to go outside, in case Ralph was also waiting in one of the parked cars on the block. Mickey stood on the side-walk in front of the handball courts with his hands in his pockets, looking around, rocking from side to side, trying to keep warm. The teenagers, about twenty yards away, were laughing and yelling and didn't seem to notice Mickey or the cold. After waiting for about another fifteen minutes, Mickey wondered if he'd made a mistake about the meeting time.

Finally, Mickey decided, To hell with it, and he headed back toward his car. As he was opening the door he heard someone whistle behind him. Mickey saw the shadow of a person around the corner on East Seventeenth, behind the fence surrounding the handball courts.

Mickey headed back across the street, gradually making out Ralph's figure.

When Mickey came up to Ralph, Ralph lunged at him, grabbing him by the shoulders and then pushing him face-first against the fence.

"What the fuck?" Mickey said.

Ralph started frisking Mickey, patting down his arms, waist and down each leg. Then he reached under Mickey's jacket and shirt and felt his chest and back.

"What the hell're you doing?" Mickey said.

Ralph didn't answer. Ralph felt Mickey's ass and reached under between Mickey's legs and squeezed his crotch.

"Sorry," Ralph said, "had to make sure you weren't wearing a wire. Come on, let's go for a drive."

"A drive?" Mickey said. "What for?"

"I gotta talk to you in private, away from the kids."

"They're up the block, they're not gonna hear anything," Mickey said. "Come on, I've been freezing my balls off out here, waiting for you. What do you want to talk about?"

Ralph looked over toward the teenagers, then he said to Mickey, "All right, let's go onto the courts."

Mickey followed Ralph onto the handball courts. They stopped in a spot in the middle of the courts where it was almost completely dark. The only light was from the lampposts on the street, about fifty yards away. Mickey could barely see Ralph, just a few feet in front of him.

"So the cops told me they talked to you," Ralph said.

Like after the robbery, Mickey was surprised to hear Ralph talk so clearly.

"Yeah, they did," Mickey said.

"Did you rat me out?"

"No," Mickey said. "Of course not."

Ralph waited a couple of seconds, looking over toward where the teenagers were gathered, then he said to Mickey, "The cops had me twelve hours today—one fuckin' chair. They said you were busted for robbing the fish store you work at. That true?"

"Yeah," Mickey said.

"You think that was the brightest thing in the world?" Ralph said. "Getting busted, time like this?"

"Don't worry, I didn't say anything," Mickey said.

For a long time, Ralph looked at Mickey with his lower lip hanging down, not saying anything. Mickey had a bad feeling but he wasn't sure why.

"We got a problem," Ralph finally said.

"What kind of problem?" Mickey said.

"You know Filippo shot Chris, right?"

"Yeah, he said it was an accident."

"It wasn't no accident," Ralph said.

Suddenly nauseous, Mickey said, "What're you talking about?"

"He only told you it was an accident, but it didn't happen that way. It was all over that slut Donna. Chris fucked her the night before the robbery and when they got upstairs Chris started laying into Filippo about it. Filippo started it, talking about how Chris's mother was a lousy drunk and Chris said, 'At least I know how to give your girlfriend a good fuck.' Then Filippo just fuckin' shot him. He put another bullet in the ceiling and made up the story about the other guy in the house."

"How do you know all this?" Mickey said.

"He fuckin' told me," Ralph said. "When I heard his uncle Louie wasn't in the house, I put a gun to his head and said, 'Tell me what the fuck's goin' on or you're gonna be in the river with Chris.' First he said it was an accident, then he told me the truth. But there's more. Remember the diamond ring we couldn't find? Turns out Filippo took it for

himself. Then maybe he felt bad, thinking he owes me something for everything I went through, getting rid of the body
and shit, and he comes to me the other day and goes, 'Here's
your five grand.' I go, 'What the fuck's this for?' and he tells
me how he sold the ring at a jewelry store in the city."

"Jesus," Mickey said.

"So now you see what I'm talking about," Ralph said.
"The cops, they know the ring was taken from the house,
they talked to Filippo already. Filippo might rat us both out
if we don't do something about him."

"What can we do?" Mickey said.

"We can kill him," Ralph said.

Mickey stood in the dark with the cold wind against his
face.

"What else we gonna do," Ralph said, "sit around, wait for
the cops to come?"

"Do whatever you want," Mickey said, "but leave me out
of it."

"You got no choice," Ralph said.

"Why's that?"

"If you don't help me I'll have to take Filippo out on my
own," Ralph said. "I'll have to do it sloppy, and if the cops
catch me guess who I'm gonna say helped me."

"They'd never believe you," Mickey said.

"You wanna chance that after just getting busted?" Ralph
said.

Mickey and Ralph stood there for a good ten seconds
without saying anything. Mickey was thinking how if he
hadn't put in that first bet for Angelo he wouldn't be here
right now.

"So what do you want me to do?" Mickey finally said.

"Go talk to Filippo tomorrow morning by work at the supermarket," Ralph said. "Tell him you heard he sold that ring and you want five g's. Tell him if you don't get the money you'll go to the cops. Then tell him to meet you tomorrow at midnight on the train tracks under the bridge by Flatbush Avenue."

"Why there?"

"Kids set off firecrackers and M-80s there all the time," Ralph said. "Someone hears the shots, they won't think nothing of it. Tell him you want to meet by the tracks because you think the cops might be watching your house. And when he gets there I'll come out and shoot him."

"Why do you need me?" Mickey said. "Why can't you do it alone?"

"After I put that gun to his head," Ralph said, "if I told him to meet me someplace, someplace out of the way, do you think he'd do it?"

"But why do I have to *go* there?" Mickey said. "Why can't I just tell him to meet you there?"

"You think he'd come out if he saw me there? If something goes wrong, call me. I'm listed—Ralph DeMarco, Fillmore Avenue. You call me at eight tomorrow night. I won't answer. Let the phone ring seven times and hang up. That means no, it's off. If it's on, you don't gotta do nothing—I'll just be there on the tracks waiting. After I get rid of Filippo's body, we'll pin Chris's murder, the robbery, everything on him. But, you gotta remember, when you leave your house tomorrow, make sure no cops're following you. If you see cops, forget about it, turn back. Tell Filippo the same thing.

If you see cops it's off, you go home, we set it up the next night. Got it?"

Mickey waited a couple of seconds then said, "Is that all?"

Ralph said, "Yeah," and Mickey left the handball court. He went back across Avenue K and got in his car. It took a few tries to turn on the engine. Finally, the car started and he made a U-turn. In the rearview mirror, he saw Ralph on the corner, his hands deep inside his coat pockets.

20

MICKEY CAME OUT of the shower, the skin on his back and chest bright pink. The TV stations had gone off for the night, so he turned on the radio. He was hoping the music would help him calm down, but when "Back in Black" came on he had a flashback to inside the stolen car with Ralph and Filippo when Chris's body fell against him. He unplugged the radio and flung it across the room. Blackie started barking downstairs, making a racket.

"Shut the fuck up!" Mickey yelled, but the dog wouldn't stop. Mickey stayed awake, trying to figure out what to do. He wished he was with Rhonda.

At eight o'clock, Mickey got up and drove to the luncheonette on Nostrand and I for breakfast. His throat was sore, probably from being out last night in the cold. He ate only part of his ham-and-eggs special then he went to talk to Filippo.

He drove down Nostrand Avenue toward the Waldbaum's near Kings Highway. He almost never went to this Waldbaum's, even when Chris was alive, because he didn't want to run into Filippo. But he knew that Chris and Filippo used to work early mornings together, so he figured Filippo would be there now.

He parked in the lot next to the supermarket and went inside. His face felt very hot and he decided he might have a fever.

After looking for Filippo in the front of the supermarket, near the checkout lines, he headed back, through the cereal aisle, then over past the frozen foods. He started back toward the front of the store when he heard Filippo laughing.

The laughter reminded Mickey of the time in fifth grade when Filippo had cornered him in the schoolyard and started chanting, "Mickey Mouse is a faggot, Mickey Mouse is a faggot." Dozens of kids, including girls, gathered around and joined in, the laughing and taunting getting even louder.

Mickey headed back toward the frozen foods, where the laughter had come from. Filippo was alone now, sticking prices on TV dinners.

"Filippo," Mickey said when he was a few feet away.

Filippo turned around.

"What the fuck're you doing here?"

"We gotta talk," Mickey said.

Filippo grabbed Mickey's arm and pulled him away through the swinging doors into the stockroom and pushed him back against a stack of boxes.

"You fuckin' crazy comin' here?" Filippo said. "The cops're on our asses. Somebody could see us together."

"I talked to Ralph," Mickey said. "He said you killed Chris on purpose. Is that true?"

Filippo squeezed Mickey's neck. "You want me to kill you too, you dumb bitch? Just get the fuck out of here."

Filippo choked Mickey for a few more seconds then let go. Mickey gagged, trying to breathe.

"Why'd you do it?" Mickey said. "Was it really over some girl?"

"Next time I choke you I'm not lettin' go," Filippo said.

Mickey couldn't stand looking at Filippo anymore, and he wondered if he'd done the right thing coming here.

"I came here to help you, you fuckin' idiot," Mickey said. "Ralph's pissed at you for stealing that ring. You better go talk to him and try to work it out."

"You think I give a shit about Ralph?" Filippo said.

"Talk to him," Mickey said. "Tell him you're sorry or something. I don't know."

"Why do you want to help me?" Filippo said.

"I don't want to help you," Mickey said, "but I don't want to see anybody else get killed, even you."

"Hey, Filippo, what's goin' on over there?"

The deep male voice had come from the other end of the stockroom. The voice sounded familiar to Mickey but he couldn't place it.

"Nothing," Filippo said.

"Nothing?" the man said. "Then what're you doin', going schizo, talking to yourself?"

A few seconds later, Angelo Santoro came over from behind Filippo. He was unshaven with messy hair hanging over his face, wearing jeans and a T-shirt. He was pushing a dolly stacked with boxes of tomato sauce.

Suddenly, Mickey remembered seeing Angelo walking along Kings Highway that day, only a few blocks away from the Waldbaum's.

Angelo looked uncomfortable for a few seconds, then he said, "Well, guess the cat's outta the bag now, huh?" Putting on his Mafia smile, Angelo said, "How's it goin' kid?"

Filippo started laughing and then Angelo started laughing with him. Mickey stood there, unable to move or think.

"You wanna put in another bet for us tonight?" Filippo said to Mickey.

Filippo and Angelo laughed harder, then they high-fived.

"Yeah," Angelo said. "If you don't put in my bet you're gonna disrespect my whole family."

"What's wrong, Mickey Mouse?" Filippo said. "Can't take a joke?"

"Yeah, hope we didn't hurt you too bad," Angelo said. "If the Seahawks got one more point that night I would've been even. Oh well. Guess that's just the way the ball bounces."

"I can't believe you fell for it," Filippo said to Mickey. "You were so stupid." Then he said to Angelo, "What'd you tell him your name was?"

"Angelo Santoro."

Filippo laughed, squeezing his balls.

Angelo stuck out his hand toward Mickey.

"Nice to meet you," he said. "My real name's Jimmy. Jimmy Ramos." Mickey stood still, his fists clenched at his sides. Jimmy pulled back his hand.

"He's fuckin' Puerto Rican and you thought he was in the mob," Filippo said, laughing.

"You gotta admit I wasn't bad," Jimmy said to Mickey. "Maybe I shoulda gone to acting school. Coulda been the next Al Pacino."

Putting on an Al-Pacino-in-*Scarface* accent, Jimmy said, "Okay, fuck you, how's 'at?"

"Hey, gimme some credit too," Filippo said. "I told you Mickey was stupid enough to fall for it."

"Sorry if I hurt you with that punch in the gut," Angelo said to Mickey, "but I had to make it look real. That's what they call Method acting, right?"

"What family did you say you was with?" Filippo said.

"Colombo," Jimmy said.

"Colombo!" Filippo said. "That's a fuckin' riot!"

Jimmy and Filippo laughed, high-fiving again.

"I better get back to work," Jimmy said, catching his breath, his face pink. Then he said to Mickey, "See you around, kid."

When Jimmy was gone Filippo said, "So you got anything else to tell me, or you gonna get the fuck out of here?"

Mickey was going to walk away, let Ralph kill Filippo, then he had a better idea.

"I want five grand," Mickey said.

"Excuse me?" Filippo said.

"I know that's how much you have left over from the ring," Mickey said. "I want all of it—tonight at midnight."

"You fuckin' high?" Filippo said.

"If you don't bring me the money I'm going to the cops.

I'll tell them everything—about the robbery, how you killed Chris—"

"Little piece of shit," Filippo said. "I'll break your fuckin' faggot head open."

"Midnight on the train tracks by the Flatbush Avenue tunnel," Mickey said. "If you're not there I'm going to the cops."

As Mickey stormed away, out of the stockroom, Filippo called after him, "Wait, get the fuck back here," but Mickey kept walking.

Heading back toward the front of the supermarket, Mickey saw Jimmy coming toward him. They stopped, facing each other.

"Hey, don't blame me," Jimmy said, holding up his hands. "It was Filippo's idea, not mine."

Mickey continued down the aisle, elbowing Jimmy hard in the ribs as he passed by. Jimmy lost his balance and stumbled against the shelves of tomato sauce. Mickey heard Jimmy screaming and jars smashing on the floor, but he left the supermarket without looking back.

21

MICKEY DROVE OUT of the Waldbaum's parking lot with his foot all the way down on the gas. When he got home he went right to the phone in the kitchen and called Vincent's Fish Market. Harry answered and Mickey hung up. He waited an hour and called again. This time Charlie said, "Vincent's Fish."

"Charlie, it's Mickey. I know Harry's there today, but can you come to my house after work? I need a favor."

AT A FEW minutes before eight, Mickey called Information and got the number for Ralph DeMarco on Fillmore Avenue. Then, at exactly eight, he dialed the number, let it ring seven times, and hung up.

The rest of the evening, Mickey stayed in his room. Although he hadn't eaten since breakfast he didn't have an appetite. He kept rehearsing the plan over and over in his head, positive it would work. At a quarter to twelve he left his apartment. Usually Blackie started barking like crazy when Mickey went down the stairs, but tonight the old dog didn't make a sound.

It was another cold night, but it wasn't as windy as it had been lately and Albany Avenue was still and quiet. Shivering, Mickey got in his car. It took a few tries on the ignition before the engine caught, and then he drove away toward Avenue J.

As Mickey turned onto Flatbush Avenue he was still shivering. Feeling his warm forehead with the back of his wrist, he wondered if he had a fever.

Passing Avenue I, Mickey realized that he had forgotten to make sure the cops weren't following him. He slowed down and pulled over to the right, looking around and back through his rearview mirror. A couple of cars had been directly behind him, but they kept going and were soon out of view. Mickey sat in his car, leaning forward, close to the heating vent, which seemed to be blowing out cold air. Finally he decided he hadn't been tailed, and he continued along Flatbush.

He pulled into a spot, right before the bridge over the train tracks, and got out of the car. Growing up, he used to play on the tracks sometimes. On the Fourth of July, he and Chris would enter through a hole in the fence near Albany Avenue, and Chris would set off his stash of illegal fireworks. Once in a while, a freight train would come by. When Mickey was eight or nine, he used to imagine hopping on board one of the trains and going someplace far away, like California or Florida. Mickey remembered how disappointed he had been when Chris explained that the

Long Island Railroad freight train tracks didn't lead to any-where much farther than Eastern Brooklyn and Queens.

Mickey used to enter the tracks through a hole in the fence farther up, near Albany Avenue, but he wasn't sure how to get there from Flatbush. He walked past the dark Sizzler restaurant on the far side of the tracks, looking over his shoulder, and then he continued past the restaurant parking lot. He was exhausted and slightly dizzy. It was get-ting darker, away from the lights on the street, and he wished he'd brought a flashlight.

At the far end of the parking lot, he spotted a small hole in the bottom of the fence and he decided he could make it through. He crouched down and went in headfirst. The ground on the other side of the fence slanted down steeper than he expected, and his hands slipped. He managed to push himself back up when something sharp on the bottom of the fence jabbed through his jeans into the back of his right leg. He started to scream, then he checked himself, not wanting to make any noise. It felt like a nail, or some-thing just as sharp sticking out of the fence, had punctured him, but he didn't think he was bleeding badly. Biting down on his lower lip, trying not to feel the pain, he managed to wriggle his way under.

He made his way slowly and carefully down the steep, frozen ground. He had forgotten how dirty the tracks and the area around them were. He stepped on beer bottles, tires, hubcaps, plastic bags, and other garbage; at one point, he thought he felt a rat pass over his right foot.

When he reached the tracks he saw Filippo standing with his hands by his sides in front of the entrance to the tunnel.

He was wearing his khaki army jacket and the dim orange light from the avenue above was shining down on him. The jacket had a lot of pockets and Mickey figured he had a gun in one of them. Mickey put his left hand in his pocket, squeezing the handle of Charlie's .38 Special.

"You got my money?!" Mickey yelled.

"Yeah!" Filippo yelled back.

"Lemme see it," Mickey said.

As Filippo reached into his pocket Mickey squeezed Charlie's gun tighter, then Filippo's hand came out with a wallet. He opened it, held up some bills. Mickey drew Charlie's gun and aimed it at Filippo.

"Put your hands up and leave the money right there," Mickey said.

"Ooh, big shot, got a gun," Filippo said.

"I'm serious," Mickey said. "Drop the money and put your fucking hands in the air!"

"All right, all right," Filippo said. "Chill out."

Filippo dropped the wallet and the bills on the ground.

"Hands in the air!" Mickey yelled.

Smiling, Filippo raised his hands.

"Back up," Mickey said.

Filippo backed up a few paces and stopped.

"All the way to the tunnel," Mickey said.

Filippo continued to back away and he stopped right near the tunnel's entrance.

The pain in Mickey's leg was getting worse. Still aiming the gun, he started to walk slowly, straight ahead, watching for any movement, but Filippo just stood there, perfectly still. As Mickey got closer, Filippo smiled wider. It was the same smile Mickey had seen at the supermarket today and so many times before.

Mickey stopped, still aiming the gun at Filippo's head, but it was starting to shake in his sweaty hand.

"What're you gonna do, shoot me?" Filippo said. "Ooh, look how scared I am. You can't shoot me. You're too much of a faggot. Come on, you little dick-sucker, let's see you do it. Come on, I want it so bad!"

Mickey wanted to make that sick smile disappear forever, but he couldn't pull the trigger. Keeping the gun aimed, he continued along the tracks toward the money.

"I knew you couldn't do it," Filippo said. "You little fuckin' faggot. You pussy."

Mickey reached the wallet and realized there were only a bunch of dollar bills on the ground.

"Where's the five grand?" Mickey said.

"Up your faggot ass," Filippo said.

A gunshot rang out from behind Filippo, from inside the tunnel. Mickey ducked and when he looked up Filippo was aiming a gun too, about to shoot. Mickey had never used a gun before—he'd never even held one before this afternoon—and he fired a wild shot, the backfire jerking his arm back high in the air. Filippo's shot whizzed by Mickey's head. Then another shot came from inside the tunnel and Filippo went down.

Mickey turned and ran toward the hill as fast as he could. He was disoriented and he wasn't sure he was running in the right direction. Someone was still shooting at him and Mickey kept his head down, telling himself if he made it to the hill he would have a chance. It was darker by the hill.

"Ralph, you fuckin' dick," Filippo groaned.

Mickey started to look back over his shoulder when he heard another shot. Keeping his head down, he ran, feeling no pain. The hill was only a few feet away and Mickey was thinking about the hole under the fence, hoping he was in the right spot to reach it. Mickey tripped over something, maybe a railroad tie, and fell, his right knee hitting the ground. He managed to get up and continue climbing, grabbing onto weeds and garbage and whatever else he could grab to keep his balance. Behind him, Ralph's footsteps and heavy breathing seemed closer, and Mickey kept going, praying the hole in the fence would be there.

At the top of the hill, Mickey bent down and felt around in the dark, but he couldn't find the opening. He heard Ralph behind him, gasping. Mickey decided he was in the wrong spot, he would never find his way out and Ralph would kill him.

Mickey was about to give up when, right in front of him, he found the opening. He started crawling through but Ralph was behind him now, probably a few feet away. Mickey turned and fired. He heard a deep, aching groan and then a heavy body tumbling down toward the train tracks. A few seconds later there was silence.

With his face close to the ground, Mickey made it through under the fence, and he continued toward Flatbush Avenue. He reached his car and started the engine. He made a U-turn—just missing a speeding van—and drove away. He wanted to go home, get into bed, and pretend this night had never happened, then he realized he was still holding Charlie's gun. He was about to pull over at a corner, figuring he'd drop the gun down a sewer grate, but he decided it was too risky. There were two people shot, maybe dead, on the train tracks, and the gun that had shot Ralph wasn't there. The police would comb the entire area looking for it.

Flatbush Avenue seemed like it was spinning, and Mickey had to squeeze the steering wheel to keep the car straight. He remembered the sound Ralph's body made when it landed on the bottom of the hill and Filippo moaning, "Ralph, you fuckin' dick." Ralph had obviously set Mickey and Filippo up, maybe hoping to make it look like they'd shot each other.

At Avenue U, Mickey made a sharp right, past the Kings Plaza shopping mall, and he pulled into a parking space. He got out of the car, looked up and down the deserted sidewalk, and continued past a small burned-out building. When he could see the water of the Jamaica Bay inlet, with the orange lights of the lampposts flickering on the surface, he threw the gun as far as he could, hearing it splash maybe twenty yards away.

When he got back in his car Mickey realized he had only made things worse. He had gotten rid of the gun, but if Ralph lived he'd tell the cops that Mickey had shot him. Mickey could say it was self-defense, but the cops would never believe it. Dumping the gun made him look as guilty as hell.

Mickey sat in the car with his head resting against the steering wheel for a long time, trying to think. Finally, he started the car and headed back toward Flatbush. He drove to East Twenty-third Street and pulled into Rhonda's driveway. The lights inside the house were out, but there was a floodlight shining along the side of the house. He went up the stoop and rang the bell, deciding that the first words he'd say to her would be, I'm sorry. If she loved him the way he knew she did, she would have to forgive him.

After waiting awhile, Mickey rang the bell again. He realized it was well after midnight, probably close to one A.M., and he could be waking up Rhonda's entire family.

He rang the bell several more times, then a light in the living room went on and Mickey saw the curtains behind the front windows rustle. He rang the bell again and then he started knocking—normally at first and then banging on the door with his fists.

"Rhonda, if you're there, it's Mickey. Come on, open up. I have to see you."

He banged again.

"Come on, open the door. It's freezing out here. Please, Rhonda, please."

He rang the bell several more times.

"Come on, this isn't fair. Open the door. Please, I have to see you. Just open the door."

For a few minutes, Mickey continued to bang against the door and ring the bell, screaming for Rhonda to open up. Finally, he heard heavy footsteps approaching, then the door swung open. Rhonda's father was standing there, wearing a dark blue sweatsuit.

"Get the hell off my property," he said.

"I need to see Rhonda," Mickey said.

"Just get the hell out of here, you little son of a bitch!"

Mickey thought he saw Rhonda, in the shadow inside the foyer. He pushed by her father, trying to get into the house. He might've jabbed him with his elbow too because her father stumbled backward and lost his balance. Mickey looked back over his shoulder and saw her father falling down the stoop, trying to grab onto the wrought-iron railing, but missing, and landing hard on the concrete. A gash appeared on the side of his head and he was squirming, trying to get up. Rhonda's stepmother ran out of the house, screaming, rushing to her husband's side, then Mickey saw the police car pulling up to the curb. He started down the stoop when a cop came out of the passenger-side door. Mickey looked at his car in the driveway, thinking he could get to it and drive away, but then thought, What's the point?

Another cop came out of the other side of the car, and they approached Mickey together.

22

MICKEY WAS TAKEN directly to Central Booking. After he was charged with aggravated assault, he was brought down to the maze of cells. The guard put him in a cell crowded with derelicts and he sat on the floor in the corner, staring out through the bars at nothing.

Throughout the night, prisoners were added and removed from the cell, but they all left Mickey alone. But then, toward morning, Mickey was leaning his head back against the concrete wall, with his eyes closed, when he heard a man say, "Hey."

Mickey looked up and saw a homeless guy standing over him. The guy's face was nearly black, covered with dirt, and he had long, greasy hair. He was wearing ripped, filthy clothes that he'd probably found in the garbage and been wearing for weeks, and he had horrible body odor. Mickey closed his eyes again and turned away, hoping the guy would leave him alone.

"I said hey," the guy said. "Why won't you look at me?"

"Go away," Mickey said.

"Hey," the guy said, "what's your name?"

Mickey didn't answer.

"I said what's your name? Huh? What's your name?"

Mickey turned farther away. Several seconds went by and Mickey knew the guy wasn't gone because he could still smell him. Then Mickey felt warm liquid on his head and the back of his neck and guys in the cell started laughing. Mickey stood up and ran to another side of the cell as the homeless guy chased after him, holding his penis between his thumb and forefinger, continuing to pee. A guard came and took the homeless guy out to another cell, and Mickey was given some paper towels to clean up with.

In the morning, Mickey refused the rolls-with-butter breakfast. He just sat in the corner, waiting to be taken out of his misery. He didn't know what was taking the detectives so long. If Ralph and Filippo were dead, their bodies should've been discovered by now.

Around noon, Mickey's lawyer showed up. He said his name was Alan Greenberg. He was a tall, very thin guy with curly brown hair. He was probably about thirty, but he seemed much older.

Greenberg sat across from Mickey in the cell and opened a little spiral notebook.

"So it looks like you've been pretty busy lately," Greenberg said. "Grand larceny, questioned about a robbery and murder, and now you're in for aggravated assault. What're you gonna do next?"

Mickey looked away. He didn't feel like talking to some smart-ass lawyer when it was only a matter of time until he was charged with murder.

"Don't look so down," Greenberg said. "The guy you assaulted needed some stitches, but he's already home from the hospital. If you plead guilty, and I suggest that you do because his wife saw the whole thing, you'll have to wait a few months for a trial date. If you're a good boy you'll get off with time served. As for the grand larceny charge, I'll have to talk to the D.A., but there wasn't much money involved, so I think we could get that reduced to petty larceny and you should get off on probation, community service, something like that. You should be out on the street ready to assault somebody else in four months tops."

Mickey was looking away.

"What's the matter," Greenberg said, "no sleep last night? It's kind of hard when you're getting peed on. I heard."

"Can you just leave me the hell alone?" Mickey said.

"Easy," Greenberg said. "It's not the end of the world. You're just lucky that guy wasn't more seriously injured—then you could be looking at a few years. I have some other good news for you—it looks like you're off the hook for that whole Manhattan Beach thing."

Mickey looked at Greenberg for the first time since he'd come into the cell.

"What're you talking about?" Mickey said.

"I just heard about it upstairs before I came down here," Greenberg said. "Some guy Castellano was found dead on the LIRR freight train tracks this morning."

"Filippo Castellano?" Mickey said.

"That's it," Greenberg said.

"What happened to him?" Mickey asked.

"He was shot," Greenberg said.

"So why am I off the hook?" Mickey asked.

"Ralph DeMarcus shot him," Greenberg said.

"You mean DeMarco," Mickey said.

"Whatever," Greenberg said. "They arrested him leaving the tracks. He had a broken leg or foot or something—he was still holding the murder weapon. He's in the hospital now, but they already booked him."

Mickey remembered shooting Ralph last night and the loud groan Ralph had made. The shot could've missed and Ralph could've just stumbled down the hill.

"You sure you heard that right?" Mickey asked.

"Positive," Greenberg said. "Why? Don't tell me you were involved in this too?"

Mickey realized that even if he hadn't shot Ralph, it didn't make a difference. Ralph had been caught and he was going to rat on Mickey for the robbery, if he hadn't already.

"What if I was?" Mickey said.

Greenberg stared at Mickey then said, "You're not kidding, are you?"

"What do you care?" Mickey said.

"Look," Greenberg said, "if you want to help yourself you'll tell me exactly what you know."

Figuring it didn't make a difference anymore, Mickey told Greenberg everything about the robbery, and how Filippo had shot Chris, and everything that had happened on the train tracks.

When Mickey was through talking, Greenberg said, "Maybe it's not as bad as you think."

"What're you talking about?" Mickey said. "Ralph knows I was at the robbery."

"So, he didn't rat you out already, what makes you think he will at all? He's got nothing to gain by fingering you. Besides, I took a look at his rap sheet. He's gone away for robbery before, so the D.A. won't let him cut a deal this time. Even if Ralph did talk, why would anybody listen? He's the one they were after, not you."

"So you really think I'll be out of here in a few months?" Mickey asked.

"If you're smart and keep your mouth shut," Greenberg said. "If the cops want to talk to you about last night, make sure I'm in the room with you and play dumb. But I really doubt they'll give you a hard time. Like I said, DeMarco was their man and they got him."

Mickey was thinking it through—three months in jail then he could get a job, save up, start taking accounting classes in the fall.

"You feeling okay?" Greenberg asked.

"I'm fine," Mickey said. "Hey, don't I get to make a phone call?"

As the guard led him down the corridor, Mickey was still imagining the future. At twenty-four, he'd have his C.P.A. license and he'd be making forty a year. He'd be living in the city, in a great apartment on a high floor, with a view of Brooklyn in the distance.

In the calling room, the guard unlocked Mickey's hand-cuffs and said, "Go ahead."

Mickey dialed the number excitedly and said into the phone, "Hi, is Rhonda there?"